A note from t...

Please be aware that my books are written with a lot of swears and smut!

Hi everyone, I am Frances, and I love writing. I am based in Nottinghamshire, England. I have two beautiful girls, a naughty dog and my wonderful husband. I have been in Education as a TA, teacher or tutor for twelve years. When I have a spare moment, or my mind starts to wander, I quickly write/type the ideas down, as you never know when inspiration can strike to create those new characters or exciting stories. I love reading and getting lost in romance novels, but I love writing them more. I hope you enjoy reading my books, and any feedback is welcome.

Let's be friends!

Don't forget to follow me on Instagram: http://www.instagram.com/francesfleurauthor

Don't forget to follow me on Facebook: https://www.facebook.com/hbpublishinghouse

Don't forget to follow me on TikTok: https://www.tiktok.com/@hbpublishinghouse

Visit: www.hbpublishinghouse.co.uk

The Purple Hearted Series

Book 1: The First – Cora and Zach's Story – Part 1 (Released March 2023)

https://mybook.to/Vyyjlxn

Book 2: And the Second – Cora and Zach's Story – Part 2 (Released May 2023)

https://mybook.to/WLMatL

Book 3: That Day – Sophie and Oliver's Story (Released July 2023)

https://mybook.to/SxuK

Book 4: Unforgettable – Daisy and Taron's Story – Part 1 (Released October 2023)

https://mybook.to/DHStYjE

Book 5: I Have to Let You Go – Trinity and Adam's Christmas Novella (Released November 2023)

https://mybook.to/ISAYk

Book 6: Never Again – Daisy's Story – Part 2 (Released May 2024)

I Have To Let You Go

Go

A Winter Novella

Frances Fleur

Contents

1. Goodbye - Adam   1

2. The rehearsal - Trinity   4

3. The call - Adam   7

4. You can't be here - Trinity   11

5. A few drinks - Adam   15

6. The first show - Trinity   19

7. The first show - Adam   23

8. Another day another city - Trinity   27

9. The morning after - Adam   31

10. The Christmas Market - Adam   35

11. The kiss - Trinity   40

12. Adam - Sadness   46

13. Trinity - Another City   50

14. The call - Adam   54

15. The dinner - Trinity   59

16. Another show - Adam   64

17. The parents - Trinity   68

18. The dinner - Adam   73

19. The morning after - Trinity   77

20. It was a mistake - Adam   81

21. I need time - Trinity   84

22. The last show - Trinity   87

23. The last show - Adam   91

24. Christmas Eve - Trinity   94

25. Christmas Eve - Adam   98

26. Christmas Day - Trinity   102

27. Christmas Day - Adam   104

28. And they lived happily ever after?   107

Acknowledgements   108

Goodbye - Adam

LINKIN PARK – GOOD GOODBYE

I brush the tears away angrily as I walk away from The Ritz Hotel in London. I just sat through the shittest day of my life ever. I don't even think I am exaggerating. I do a quick mental think of all the shittest days of my life, and yep, this was it. The girl I have been best friends with and also totally in love with for the last six years just got married...to someone else.

A black Hackney carriage drives by the entrance and I stick my hand out. This is going to cost me a bomb, but I don't care. I can't ride the tube in my state; someone will think I'm a madman, although right now they're not far from the truth; I feel insane - not that I care what people think. But what I do know right now is that I need to be so drunk I forget today. I want to wake up tomorrow face down in a ditch somewhere, suffocating in my own vomit because I want to black out today and forget it ever existed. I want to forget her, forget my years wasted on her, thinking she would change her mind. All the times I was there to comfort her, be the nice guy – not anymore. I want to erase Cora Wilkinson from my brain and squash our memories together like a bug.

"Where to, mate?" the taxi driver asks as I climb into the backseat.

"Soho," I reply. The driver nods. I'm glad it's dark. I know my eyes are rimmed red from crying. I dial Charlie, and he answers in one ring.

"I'm surprised you lasted that long," he jokes. I clear my throat, hoping to take the edge off my wavering voice.

"Well, I did, and she still married him," I hear him sigh, and I'm almost surprised he doesn't say I told you so, which I'm grateful for when he doesn't.

"I know, and I'm sorry...my set is next. Come watch me play, and then I will get you shit-faced. I think it's time you get over Cora for real. Get your cock wet; that is what works for me! Look, I will see you in a bit; I gotta go warm up."

With that, he's gone. I mull over his words. I wish it were that simple. I want to forget her, but she had a wonderful way of being so kind and crawling back into my head and fantasy land. I was a goner the first day I met her at university, with the way her laugh lit up the room, her perfect hair and face, the passion she has for music, especially when she plays the piano on stage and her mind is just extraordinary...

Stop this, you idiot!

I want to mentally strangle myself because, for some reason, my stupid brain could not get it in my head that she is with someone else and has been for the last five years. When we first met at university, she was quiet and reserved. I liked that about her as it reminded her of who I am. I've never been one to be the centre of attention; I like to sit back and observe, and when I need to speak, I will. She seemed the same, but I found out it was due to a recent heartbreak, a 'Zach', the same chump she had just married.

They had split up, not that I wanted to be a rebound, but she had that personality, body and beauty that pulled me into her space, and I couldn't have stopped myself even if I wanted to. When we finally kissed that November, I really thought I had met someone who understood me, who saw me. We kissed a lot and messed around in the bedroom, although we never slept together. I wanted to so bad, and my dick ached for her. But I am respectful and patient. I would never rush a person into anything they did not want to do. Months went by, she had a bereavement within the family, and I was a shoulder to cry on, a great friend; I was there for her whenever she needed me.

But then Zach returned and everything changed. She didn't need me anymore, I was like a fart in the wind, insignificant and already forgotten. But I held on tight; it didn't help that we were on the same course for another two years, and I'm terrible at confrontation. So, I sucked it up; I remained her best friend still, minus the kissing. She had 'the talk' with me, and I assured her I was fine, but I wasn't. I held on to the hope that maybe she would finally see me and want to be with me. But, instead, each day, I slowly suffocated in fantasy land whilst my heart cracked a little each time I saw them together. Today, when they finally married, my heart shattered into a million pieces.

I loosen my tie on my suit and brush away another tear, thinking of all those years I wasted on Cora Wilkinson.

But not anymore. Fuck her, fuck women and most of all fuck being the nice guy.

The rehearsal - Trinity

Backstreet Boys – Christmas Time

Three months later

Day 1 of rehearsal, and I'm oddly nervous. I know the musical notes off by heart with my eyes closed; it is one of the stipulations for today. For the last three months, I have rehearsed my arse off in my little flat – the neighbours could probably do a rendition of it too, not that they complained. I was back-to-back with two old people - they love listening to me practice, thank goodness.

Today, all of the band are together in a stuffy, run-down theatre in the heart of London. We only have a few days to rehearse, so we have to work together as a team, note each other's timing, and, most of all, get on with the conductor because if he's out of time, we are all screwed. The band is small, only fourteen of us - they all seem friendly, so that's a bonus. It's always a bit crappy if you work with a travelling orchestra and end up with stuck-up entitled snobs, but I learned quickly what circles they gravitated to and stayed away from those. It's not worth the hassle, the mental energy or the money.

After a few days of rehearsing, the actors will come in, and we get another few days to rehearse with them, too, and then we are off on tour. I am buzzing with excitement; I need a break from London and all its chaos, a different kind of winter. But playing a musical instrument with this particular show comes with the bonus of travelling around England at Christmas time. Usually, Christmas consists of me, my parents, and my younger brother and all that is great, but I have spent all 24 Christmases with them and this year, I want one on my own, being independent and doing something awesome.

The thought of not having to listen over Christmas dinner to how little brother Will was doing, how great he was, and what cases he was solving, felt oddly relieving. I would be able to bypass the comments from my parents about why (even after a very expensive university course) I have only landed low-key roles – which, by the way, paid the bills and made me very happy. Why, they would comment, have I spent all my money on a university course that didn't deliver?

But it did deliver. It delivered to my soul.

My parents were practical people, having worked in office jobs all their lives and paid every month the same amount of money. Don't get me wrong, they are lovely and supportive in their own way. They've come to every show I've ever been in, and I grew up not wanting. But because I wasn't making the typical wage, they couldn't understand what I was doing wrong and why I wasn't applying for better roles because I was so talented. I had to consistently remind them that freelance work comes in spots, and I apply to jobs that I feel passionate about. But they didn't get it; they would mumble that work isn't about passion, it's about getting paid and supporting yourself. They didn't complain much, but I could see the disappointment in their eyes or their extra gush at Will for getting another promotion.

Yawn, boring!

An office job sounded cramped and mundane. I like the thrill of the music, the new notes to learn, meeting new people and watching new plays or concerts. It made me feel alive; I lived for the arts. So what if I wasn't getting thousands upon thousands of pounds every month? I'm working for something that makes me happy - I don't think it's something they will ever understand.

The morning rehearsal goes by quickly; everyone seems to complement each other in their musical style. I think the next three weeks travelling with this group of people is going to be great.

At lunch, I grab a quick roll from the sandwich shop on the corner and fire a text off to my best friend Cora, saying rehearsal is going well. She responds with a thumbs up; I know she is busy finishing off her tour with the London Orchestra, but we promise to catch up after Christmas.

As I enter the shabby rehearsal space, I can hear the director shouting a lot of profanities in the auditorium. I'm unsure what to do. Should I leave, walk by and pretend I can't hear him, or ask what's wrong? I don't even get a chance to make my mind up before he's storming towards me.

"Well, fucking great!" he barks.

"Is everything okay?" I sound meek, and that annoys me. I clear my throat and stand taller to try and rescue the situation.

"No, Trinity, everything is NOT okay. Bloody Darren has broken his shitting finger messing about at lunch and now we are down a guitarist. Fuck!" he stomps his foot like an angry child and walks past me and out of the auditorium, slamming the door so hard I think it might shatter the glass.

Well, crap, that puts a spanner in the works!

The call - Adam

CHER - BABY PLEASE COME HOME

I trail soft kisses down Liv's back. I met her in a bar last night, I had gone out with Charlie; in fact, I go out most nights with Charlie unless I'm away working. I love drinking, dancing, letting off steam and finding a woman to kiss, touch and, most importantly, make her moan my name over and over again in my bed. Liv is good, really good at giving head, where my dick goes right to the back of her mouth and she gags; the vibration and noise are sexy as hell. Not only is she great with her mouth, but she's a frigging firecracker in the bedroom, all the positions, back, front, floor, bed, and door. It had been a wild and exhausting night. But she would need to leave soon, and I want one more taste of her. She groans at my contact. I know she's asleep, but I can also see it's just after midday and usually, I don't like people in my house past then. But she had kept me up all night, so she is worth a little flexibility, like her legs. I roll her onto her back.

"Adam, I'm sleeping," she mutters, still half asleep.

"And I'm not," I continue my soft kisses down her body and reach the sweet spot. I swirl my tongue around her nub and suck down gently; she tastes delicious, she moans at my action, and I look up and see her gaze on me under her hooded eyes. I swirl my tongue in a rhythmic motion, back and forth, and her moans become louder. I insert a finger, and she bucks off the bed; she's wet and ready, but not yet. I like it just at the point when she's almost coming, and I slam into her balls deep – it's the best feeling. My cock perks up – I'm ready now. I want to push deep into her soft body and come hard, and then I need to get on with my day.

My phone buzzes, but it can wait. I'm almost at the sweet bit; she's moaning and muttering, she's close, I can feel it. My phone buzzes again. I look over but can't quite see who's calling, plus my contacts are out and my glasses are somewhere else - so I wouldn't see the caller display anyway.

Fuck. It could be important.

I quickly weigh up the options, an important phone call or another round of fucking. It is close, so close. But when the phone buzzes again, I give in because if it's one of my sisters, then I won't hear the fucking end of it and that is much worse than pissing off Liv and not making her come.

I sigh, stop, and answer the phone whilst wiping my fingers on my boxers.

"Hello?" I see Liv sit up. Her face is angry. I shrug and stick my finger up, asking her to wait a minute. She gives me a look as if to say - what the hell, flings herself off the bed and slams my bathroom door shut.

"Adam, it's me, Elijah," he sounds stressed, but then again, he always does. Elijah is an up-and-coming theatre director. We've worked on several projects together over the years, and he's always been a laugh. We've kept in contact and had several drinks and dinners out, putting the world to rights, and he drinks me under the table every time.

"What's up, mate? The rehearsals start today, right?" I try to sound cheerful and start thinking about how I can sweet-talk Liv into coming back to bed.

"They were until Darren bloody broke his finger, and now, we are down a guitarist," he moans.

"Oh no, I know where this is going," I mutter.

"I wouldn't ask if I weren't desperate," he sighs.

"Cheers."

"You know what I mean, dipshit. Most of these musicians have had the sheet music for months; you have the talent just to pick it up and do it exceptionally well. Why you haven't accepted any of those deals is beyond me. But yet here I am, grateful you are such a stubborn shit and are available for my Christmas show." I sigh, scrubbing my hands over my face.

Liv emerges from the bathroom, clothed, with a full-on scowl, and she gives me the one-finger birdie. I almost call out and tell her to wait, but for what – I want her to go soon anyway. "So, what I am saying," Elijah continues, "please come save me from this shitty predicament I am in and help a pal out."

I hear the door slam.

Bye, Liv, the sex was great.

"Eli, I really don't know," I admit.

"Adam, I know you are having some personal crisis, but so am I. Plus, if you're still on the mantra of shagging every bird you see to get over what's her face, then what better way to do it than a city-to-city tour. New girl, different town, proper musician, bad boy."

I chuckle. I sound like a horrible person, but getting my dick wet most nights did help. I hadn't thought about Cora so desperately in weeks. A few weeks away from home might do me good. I had been a moody shit for ages, and being with Elijah was always a good laugh.

"Fine, but you owe me, and I get your hotel room, and I'm riding with you, not on the crappy tour bus," I say, sounding pissed off, but really, I know it will be fun.

"Deal, get your ass down to Marylebone ASAP; we are at the auditorium," he hangs up without another word.

Guess that's my December sorted then, and here I was thinking I would have a restful Christmas...guess not. I hope my liver is ready for the all-night partying.

You can't be here - Trinity

ARIANA GRANDE – SANTA TELL ME

We have run through another set this afternoon, minus the guitarist, but it's been okay. The nerves have settled down a little, and Elijah, the director, seems to be less angry. So, I assume he has got a replacement until I realise who the replacement is.

Adam Turner.

My best friend from university, the guy I have been secretly in love with since the day we met, comes striding onto the stage like he owns the world. I haven't seen him for quite a few weeks; he never fails to steal my breath. His hair is all combed into a side parting, and he's lost his Clarke Kent glasses - he must have got contacts. He clenches his strong jaw, and his muscles flex in his tight t-shirt. I need to stop looking because if I'm not careful, I will be a messy puddle on the floor with all this dribbling.

I internally sigh.

But he never used to be like this, with his confident walk and 'the look' he gives everyone that tells you he thinks he's the greatest thing since sliced bread. He used to be reserved and thoughtful, not the cocky shit he's turned into since ... since Cora got married.

He's rung me several times drunk; he never mentions her but always lets me know he's having a great time. Or he plasters himself over social media working out or showing he's at another club, kissing someone else that's not me. I even went round to his house once, and another person was there, naked. I left quickly and felt so upset I don't think he even noticed. I knew right then I had to start to distance myself. I couldn't cope seeing him faun over my best friend, Cora, for five years, and I certainly can't take him sleeping with every woman in London and be okay with it.

Adam has changed into someone I didn't even recognise, a person I didn't like anymore – well, that's what I'm telling myself. He'd become the bad, unobtainable guy that every woman and their dog wanted. But despite all this, despite him spreading himself over every girl he can, my heart still does a little happy dance that he's here. Until the realisation of WHY he's here comes crashing down onto me and chucks an ice-cold bucket of water over my body.

Bugger.

He shakes Elijah's hand and stares over the rest of us on the other side of the stage. He hasn't seen me yet. I wonder if I could hide or run away like a screaming mad woman. The thought that he's here and joining the show makes me shiver, as I know what that means. It means I will have to be near him every day for three weeks, and there's no escaping to my dorm room or back home to cry about him like I did at university. It will be me and him day in and day out for three weeks.

I don't know how this is going to work.

I can't keep my feelings in check the whole time I am on this Christmas tour. I don't think I am strong enough for that. And in my head, I let myself play out a fantasy: I throw my violin on the ground, it obviously smashes into pieces, I tell everyone to screw themselves, and I walk out. Also, in that fantasy, Adam declares that he's always loved me, and we share the most romantic kiss I have ever experienced in my life.

But it doesn't happen. I don't leave because I need the money. I have also already signed a contract, so unless I die at this precise minute or break my finger like Darren, then it's tough! The director, Elijah, waves his hands in the air, and the conductor tells us to stop playing.

"Everybody, can I have your attention, please," a slither of hope creeps in that he's not the replacement, and he's just here for the day – until the real guitarist arrives. Then Adam's handsome eyes land on mine, and he realises I'm here too. He then cocks an eyebrow, a questioning look and then a panty-wetting smile spreads across his face. I give him a small wave as I put my bow and violin down to one side. I feel a small blush creep up my neck; he always affects me – thank goodness I wore a jumper today.

The lady leans in next to me and whispers, "He's fit; I was getting worried there'd be no eye candy; Christmas has come early. Thank you, Santa," I chuckle and nod, unsure of what to say or let her know that Adam and I have been friends for years because she's not wrong. He is gorgeous. Even more so in the last year or two since he took himself to the gym. He's filled out in all the right places and is now all pure muscle.

I've seen his pictures on social media, where his top is off in the gym. Yes, I looked, yes, I definitely looked more than a few times, and I may have also printed out the picture and stuck it to my fridge door to help wake me up in the mornings – it may have got me through a few lonely nights, too.

"Thank you," Elijah continues, "this is Adam, the replacement for Darren - the dipshit. Adam is an excellent, well, everything, and we are honoured to have him here in our show, so please make him feel welcome." Some people clap, some people wave and say hi, and the girl next to me is flapping like a frigging bird. I almost expect to see a flash of boobs with her ridiculous display.

I'm slightly annoyed that he is here because this Christmas show was about me exploring myself, coming off social media for a bit and away from my life in London. More importantly, away from him, and the one person I really wanted to get away from is here. I only told Cora about the tour, not Adam, not even my parents, really. I want something for myself, but it looks like fate has other plans.

Thanks a lot!

I look up at him, meeting his amused gaze.

"Why are you here?" I mouth.

He shrugs, grabs the guitar and settles into his seat. I can't help but roll my eyes. So, I guess this is happening then.

Adam Turner, you suck!

A few drinks - Adam

THE POGUES – FAIRYTALE OF NEW YORK

The afternoon is pretty straightforward, with a few minor note changes, but it's nothing complicated, and the fact that Trinity is here is going to make the next three weeks so much more fun. We were close friends at university - although we've drifted apart over the years, whenever we see each other, we always pick up where we left off. What I didn't understand was why she didn't tell me she was in the Christmas show. We only spoke last month, and if what Elijah says is true, Trin has known about this for months, and she never said anything.

Odd.

Maybe she did tell me and I didn't listen? I mean, I have been a bit busy working and doing other people at the moment - so it could've slipped my mind. I shrugged the thought off, putting the guitar back on the stand and stretching my arms out. Sitting for hours is never great for me and a dull ache in my lower back has not gone unnoticed. A young girl, in her early twenties, with perky tits and a wide smile approaches me.

"Hey, I'm Lorelle, but you may call me Elle," she flutters her eyelashes a little. Don't get me wrong, if we met in a club, we definitely would, but we have three weeks of being together; I don't want a cling-on or anything that I can't get away from.

"Hi, I'm Adam, but you can call me Adam," she giggles and lightly slaps my arm. Captain Mrs Obvious here with her flirty touches; she's making it too easy. I like a challenge. I'm bored already.

"Stop, you're too funny," she giggles again. I look over her shoulder and see Trin. She rolls her eyes and walks off the stage.

"So, we are all going to the bar for drinks now. Are you coming?"

"Sure," I reply, trying to keep my voice even because I think if I give her a slight bit of interest, she'll get the wrong idea, and then I won't be able to shake her off.

"Great, I can introduce you to everyone," she links her arm with mine, which I drop immediately. I don't want to play this game and I don't need her help to be introduced, I walk ahead of her as she hurries to catch up, "So, where are you from?" Elle asks, trying to engage me in mindless chatter

"Here."

"Oh, me too, well sort of, I'm from Reading," she sounds pleased with herself, and I can't be bothered to pull her up on the fact that Reading is not in London.

I grab my coat as we exit the auditorium; even though it's late November, the weather has changed quickly from acceptable autumn to freezing my balls off for winter. I see Trinity is at the front of the group chatting with some man, and I get an odd feeling of...

Jealousy? I don't know, nah, not that.

But seeing her chatting so intimately with a man doesn't sit right in my stomach. Maybe it is the fact that I haven't eaten for hours, but she's laughing and he is too at what looks to be the funniest thing ever, and that sends weird messages to my brain.

Elle is beside me again; she's starting to remind me of a lost chick and chirps in, "Oh, that's Trinity and Ben. They both play the strings with me. They look cute together, right?" I grunt, "I heard that he's going to make his moves later," she giggles again like she's got all the inside scoop and gossip, and I hate gossipers.

We enter the bar across the street, and I hang back a moment and wait for Elijah; he claps me on the back, "How are you settling into it?"

"Fine," I reply, heading straight for the bar to order a beer, "First round is on you," he chuckles and orders the drinks. I turn and survey the room. Most of the group is sat over in the booths chatting. Trinity is still chatting with Ben with all the smiles. It shouldn't annoy me, but it does; she hasn't even said hi. And that bothers me more than it should.

Why doesn't she even acknowledge me?

Elijah goes through the schedule of the next three weeks: 14 city stops with a day off scattered here and there, some places I haven't been before, which I like. We head off early tomorrow morning. The first stop is Birmingham. After a few beers and a catch-up with Elijah, I'm feeling more relaxed. Thankfully, Elle has immersed herself in the chatter of other people, away from me. Elijah goes off to check in with the rest of the orchestra. Trinity is still closely talking with Ben; she might as well sit on his bloody knee and just like that, my mood has turned sour again. Maybe I need an early night. Ben comes to the bar and shakes my hand, "Adam, right?"

"Yep, Ben, right?"

"Yeah," he seems pleased that I know his name, and I already know I hate him. "You not coming to sit with us all?" he asks as he orders a drink. I don't know what it is about him, but even his voice is annoying. He has dark hair with a preppy dress vibe, but it doesn't suit him; it's as if he is trying too hard.

"Nah, I'm going to head home soon," I reply.

"Bit antisocial of you, don't you think? I mean, you are new to the team, too," I didn't fail to notice the undertone of sarcasm in his voice.

"I'm not here to make friends, Ben," I snarl back. He doesn't catch my tone, or if he does, he doesn't care.

"Shame, some really nice ladies here," he smirks, looking over at Trinity, who is oddly staring daggers at me. Her face looks annoyed. I don't know why she still hasn't come over to say hi.

"Oh yeah, like Trinity?" he laughs, a wet one; I ball my fists as my patience wears thin with this one.

"Yeah, I mean, she's funny, smart, and her body is fine. Let's see if she's as easy as her smiles," he mutters.

"What?" my face darkens at his remark. How dare he talk about Trinity this way? He puts his hands up in surrender, grabs the drinks, and then chuckles.

"Calm down, man, if you wanted first dibs, you should have got in there quick," he walks away as if he doesn't realise he's insulted one of my good friends. Wait. Has she not told anyone that we know each other?

Interesting.

The first show - Trinity

COLDPLAY – CHRISTMAS LIGHTS

Today is the first day of the tour. The drive up to Birmingham is quick; there is no messing on the M1. I sit with Ben, and we have a good chat about our musical styles. I like all his geeky knowledge of singers, and we chat a lot about films, too. His laugh is infectious, and we just get on really well. He's a touchy-feely guy, and to be honest, I like having the attention. I don't crave attention, but I like how freely he gives it to me.

I think about what it would be like to have sex with Ben. There's a definite attraction there and I think he might be the one to officially get me over my dry spell – it's been a long time. Although I am slightly happy that Adam is not riding with us, it means I can get to know the band I'm playing with rather than ogle and be distracted by him. Although, I also feel disappointed because I want to ogle and be distracted by him.

Flipping heck, Trinity, get your feelings in check.

Elle is disappointed too – she seems put out by Adam not being on the bus and is muttering about how he gets to ride with Elijah because he's too good to ride with the rest of us. We arrive at a modern-looking building called the Hippodrome. Although it looks nothing like a theatre, but I like small surprises like these.

The bus driver says that we are staying at the Holiday Inn a few streets up, so we leave our bags on the bus - we can check in to the hotel after our first sound check. We have two today, one with the cast before the first performance this evening - hopefully, it will all go smoothly.

I wander off the bus, sign in backstage and have a little poke around. Lots of beige cold corridors leading to different dressing rooms, cupboards of outfits and little offices greet me. I walk onto the stage, it's oddly quiet, but the set is magnificent. A winter wonderland background and hand-painted buildings. I look out onto the empty red sea of seats, the yellow squared tiled ceiling and the small golden balconies. Being in a theatre feels like home. I close my eyes and breathe it all in. I love the theatre, and I love music.

I feel him before I see him as his arms droop over my shoulders from behind, giving me a small kiss on my cheek.

"Good morning gorgeous, are you feeling hungover?" he whispers in my ear. I shudder from his close contact, almost forgetting how easy he is with his kisses and cuddles. I snap my eyes open, trying to centre myself and not fall into these easy displays of affection. I need to keep my distance. I used to crave these from him daily, anything to be close to him, and I cannot do it anymore. I pull away and turn to look at him, and I hate myself that I still fancy the crap out of him. I have done so since the first time I saw him at university; he's still so beautiful in my eyes.

"What's with the frown? Did I say something wrong?" he smirks. "Didn't big, bad-boy Ben put out?" he lowers his bottom lip, whining, and the urge to bite it feels pretty nice right now. I shake the thought away.

I need to keep my distance.

Plus, why does he care? He's never been interested in my love life, ever! Not that I have ever had a love life around him. I was too busy being in love with him even to notice anyone else.

Not anymore!

"Why? Jealous?" I also put my sulk face on and lower my bottom lip to mimic his actions. Something crosses his face quickly, and then it's gone. We stare at one another for a moment, the tension suddenly thick and then he steps back.

"Tell me something, Trin. Why didn't you tell me you got into Elijah's show?" I shrug off his comment like it's no big deal and walk to the edge of the stage. I didn't want to tell him I was running away from him or that I needed a break from his friendship to try and get over him. I wouldn't even know how to explain or where to start. Plus, I have been doing this dance for so many years and had been friend-zoned so hard that I was at the point that if we did anything now, it might ruin the friendship.

I didn't want to lose his friendship.

It's not even that we see each other much anymore - that thought alone made me feel sad. "Are you nervous about tonight?"

"I'm always nervous pre-show, aren't you?" I turn to look at him and his eyes are really staring at me; it makes my tummy do little funny dances.

"Sometimes," he takes a big breath and then looks out towards the audience. I watch him closely as he takes it all in. His sandy hair flops over his eyes and he brushes it back with his hand, showing off his very nice biceps. "I love looking out into the audience, don't you?" I nod in agreement and chuckle as I was just doing the same thing.

"Why did you stop wearing your glasses?" he thinks about my question for a moment and then turns to look at me.

"Why? Is it too much face now?" he smiles, a genuine one and I like the way his blue eyes light up and his face crinkles. I can't help but smile back at him.

"Always too much face with you," I muse back.

He shrugs, "Fancied a change, you know?" I nod in agreement.

"Things are changing, that's for sure." I agree flippantly. I can see he's going to ask what I mean by my comment - but we are interrupted.

"Right!" I turn and hear Elijah backstage, "Can everyone grab their instruments and be down in the orchestra pit in 15 minutes, let's get this show started!"

Deep breaths, I can do this!

The first show - Adam

JUSTIN BIEBER – ROCKING AROUND THE CHRISTMAS TREE

Trinity is different. I can't put my finger on it, but she is, and it feels like she's pushing me away. It hurts. I can feel our friendship slipping through my fingers, and I don't know what I have done wrong or how to fix it.

You're imagining it, asshole, as you did when you thought Cora was going to realise she was in love with you and call off her wedding - which she didn't!

I tell myself I'm not bothered, but I clearly am. I respect Trinity a lot and consider her my friend – which is saying a lot for me as I don't have any other 'girl' friends, well, not anymore anyway. I push the thought aside and bring myself back to the present. All 15 of us are squashed into the orchestra pit, we have less than 5 minutes to go, and I definitely need to take a piss.

Would people be annoyed if I finished my Coke and wee in the bottle? I will see how desperate I get.

I take a quick peek out of the pit and look out at the excited chatter of the audience. I love this bit, pre-show. No one knows exactly what it will be like as it's the first one, and people are all in high spirits due to Christmas being only a few weeks away. I inhale all their positivity and energy. The conductor tells me to sit down, and he looks furious. I do a little meerkat look, and I inwardly curse being caught out. But then I see that Ben has a smirk on his face. Just one look from him, and I am annoyed; his face annoys me.

The conductor taps, and we start the show. Over the first half, I can't help my eyes as they gravitate towards Trinity on her violin; she is biting her lip as her forehead furrows; she has her super concentrating face on. I used to remember that face at university – if you interrupted her with that face on whilst she played a movement, she would bite your head off. And when she gets lost in a piece of music like she is now, her eyes close momentarily as if she is transported to another world. She's so beautiful when she's at one with the music.

Where the hell did that thought come from?

I miss one of my notes, and the whole team glare at me.

Ops, too busy staring at Trinity.

Well, apart from Ben, he's smirking at me like a dickhole, note to self, at any opportunity, punch his face in. The rest of the first half goes off without a hitch, and as soon as the interval is on, I almost catapult out of the seat and straight to the toilet before I piss my pants. I definitely will not down a beer before the show tomorrow.

As I trot to the toilets, I hear Ben comment that I'm clearly not up to standard and can't handle it if I am rushing off to 'vom' at interval time. Game on, Ben game on!

I think I piss for a whole 2 minutes, and oh jeez, it's the best one of my entire life. I'm groaning into the urinal, having the best time. It's an utter relief. As I come out of the bathroom, Trinity is waiting outside; she looks concerned.

"You, okay?" her whole face is covered in worry for me. Her downturned eyes and the bite of her plump lips make me feel all warm inside. No one has asked if I'm okay and genuinely given a crap for a while (my sisters don't count, btw), and I am reminded how great she is as a person. I pull her into a hug and hold her close for a moment. Inhaling her floral scent, that smell transports me straight back to university when life was uncomplicated. She stands there rigidly and awkwardly pats me. "If you have a bug and have now given it to me, you're dead, Adam," I suppress a laugh and pull back, kissing her on the cheek.

"Just needed a piss Trin, but thanks for your concern," I wipe the sloppy kiss from her cheek and give her my best grin.

"I hope you washed your hands?" Without thinking, I stick my fingers in her mouth, and for a moment, I swear she sucks my fingers gently and groans. She pulls away and scrunches up her face.

"Nope," I love messing with her; she rises to the bait every time.

"You are disgusting!" she shrieks.

"But you love me, right?" I droop my arm around her and walk back to the orchestra pit. "What's the deal with big, bad boy Ben? If he was Darth Vader, I think I would have died ten times over."

She rolls her eyes and settles back down in her seat, I wink at Elle, who giggles and then stare at Ben, who is still giving me his best shit-eating grin.

"Alright there?" he asks, patting his belly, "Bit sick, were we? Bit nervous?" I didn't miss the condescending tone in his voice again.

"If you mean I downed a beer before show time and needed a piss, then yes!"

"Ew, gross," I hear Elle respond, as she listens to our conversation.

"He didn't wash his hands either!" Trinity chirps in. I look at her cheeky smile and give her my best wink.

"Dude, that's really disgusting," Ben remarks.

Like your face, I almost respond as a child. But instead, I act like one and lick my fingers individually with a pop, then pick my guitar up and tune it. I glance up at Ben quickly, who looks at me like I shat on him and then at Trinity, who is silently chuckling to herself.

Sometimes, people can't take a joke.

Another day another city
– Trinity

JACKSON 5 – I SAW MOMMY KISSING SANTA CLAUS

My head hurts, I roll over and almost puke. I drank far too much last night after the show. I groan for several moments, wishing I could sleep through this, but yep, this is coming back up. I run to the bathroom, close my eyes and eject all of the contents of my stomach, including the kitchen sink, out of my mouth until I think there's nothing left. Satisfied that I'm not going to vomit anymore, I lie down on the cool tiles of the bathroom floor. I concentrate on my breathing and try to get my heartbeat under control. I hate being sick; it makes me dizzy and sweaty, yet it seems I still haven't learned my lesson when it comes to drinking.

I think back over the last several days, and this Christmas musical tour has been amazing. From Birmingham, we went to Coventry, then to Sheffield and now we are in Nottingham. I love taking in new sights of the different cities, each one offering something different and interesting. I love playing with my orchestral team, but, mainly, I'm so glad I signed up for this tour; it makes me feel stronger and less stuck in a rut with my musical career. The Theatre Royal" in Nottingham was so beautiful to play in last night. Built in the late middle 1800s, it has large standing columns on the outside, and the inside was just as breathtaking; the decorative lighting and the yellow haze it gave felt so magical; it's definitely my favourite place to play so far.

Knowing we all had a day off today, we went out last night, and everyone was on top form. We drank, we danced, I think karaoke was in there at some point and oh... yes, I kissed Ben; in my drunken haze, I kissed him. Was he a good kisser? Maybe. I don't remember much, which sucks – stupid social drinking and, oh no, it all came flooding back like a tidal wave. I sit up like a possessed zombie and vomit into the toilet again.

Last night, we went to a bar just off the Market Square. the weather was miserable, freezing cold rain, so I don't think anyone wanted to go far from the hotel. The place we went to was like a make-shift bar / 90s-night club, which had me fired up, as I love pop music and it was all my favourite songs from my era. Ben kept putting drinks in my hand, which was fine by me. I danced until my feet hurt, laughed at everything and had the biggest smile on my face. The only thing that dampened it a little was Elle, she was all over Adam like a bad rash.

"Save me," he mouthed as Elle talked his ear off. I flipped him the bird and smirked; he could listen to her downright obsessive talking. Serves him right for being such a beautiful flirt.

Ben is being all goofy and funny - I really like spending time with him. I don't know how Adam does it, but one minute, he is with the group talking, and the next, he's on the dance floor kissing some random and very beautiful girl. My heart sank; I wanted to cry. I took a moment and let the hurt wash over me and then a deep breath.

He cannot hurt me; he is not mine and never will be; I have to get over this.

So, I did something else other than wallow about it not being me. I felt brave and forward, and I pulled Ben instead, and we kissed. He seemed happy about it. I remember there being a lot of tongues, but when I pulled away from him, Adam was literally glowering at me.

Two can play that game.

He then whispered into the girl's ear; she smiled, nodded and then they both left. I felt like my heart broke. He kissed someone else and then left with them. So, I put on my best smile and carried on drinking, dancing and kissing Ben. But my heart was crushed inside – probably why I did so many shots, too.

At some point, we ended up back at the hotel, which luckily was not far. A lot of the team came back and some went on to another club, but I could barely see or think straight. When we got back to the hotel, Ben came into my room, we kissed a hell of a lot more, we were definitely on the bed and some grinding action was going on and then, oh gosh, I vomited, and then it's a blur. I must have passed out.

Where did Ben go? Oh no, is he still here?

I pull myself up from the floor again and peek out the door; he's on my bloody bed. Looking down, I'm grateful that I'm still fully clothed. Oh gosh, what a shitty nightmare. He's snoring, I close the door, turn the shower on and get in fully clothed. I smell like vomit and I'm not carrying these clothes around with me trying to find a laundrette. I lie down in the shower and let the water wash away my hangover. I finally pull off the dress, wash my hair and brush my teeth about ten times, still tasting the acid in the back of my throat. I need a cup of tea and greasy food, fast!

I open the door slowly and see that Ben hasn't moved from the top of my bed, still fast asleep. I grab some clothes from my suitcase and he starts to stir. I go back into the bathroom and slam the door - that ought to wake him up. I feel awkward and like a bag of crap - he needs to leave so I can die in peace from my hangover. I dress quickly in leggings and a baggy jumper, braid my hair and don't even bother with make-up. I can outwardly look how I inwardly feel.

Crap.

A few minutes later, I open the door, Ben is sitting up at the end of the bed. His dark hair is in messy directions, his brown eyes look as broken as mine and his 5-o clock shadow is well past midnight. Also, I think he may have special secret powers to grow his beard hair so fast like that. He looks at me a bit sheepishly.

"How are you feeling?" he grumbles.

"Like I've died," he nods in agreement.

"Yeah, me too," he scrubs his magical beard, "Look, I'm going to be honest with you, Trinity, I don't remember much of last night as I drank far too much. I don't even remember coming back here, and I am pretty sure we didn't sleep together - seeing as I'm fully clothed." I sigh in happiness that he is feeling as shit as me and it looks like we both passed out. I'm not into drunk sex or any of that. "But I like you," he continues, "and I would like to do this again, minus the drinks and maybe dinner involved?" He looks at me expectantly.

I smile, "I think I would like that," he stands up from the bed and kisses me gently on the lips. He smells so bad I have to hold my breath a little, so I don't vomit - but who doesn't smell like a brewery after a heavy night out on the town?

"I'll catch you later," he says as he leaves my room. I groan and put on my shoes in hopes of not dying before finding some bloody food and a cure for a hangover.

The morning after - Adam

KYLIE MINOGUE – SANTA BABY

I like Nottingham. It's not a place I have visited before, being from Devon, it feels miles away. I like the seaside life, but I also love the city life that London has to offer. I stayed after graduation because it now felt like home. But Nottingham is somewhere in between, minus the sea, a city where there is a lot going on but not too much that you feel overwhelmed.

I woke up early this morning, still feeling agitated and confused by my reaction to Trinity kissing Ben last night. Elle was so touchy-feely, I felt I was more like a fine prize cow won at a show where everyone wanted to pet it - that I'd had enough. When I made contact with the fit lady on the dance floor, she gave me the eyes and a quirk of her pretty lips that showed she was interested. I returned with a small nod in appreciation, walked over and kissed her. If that wasn't a 'piss off I'm not interested in you Elle' I don't know what else I could have done. The kiss was nothing to write home about, but it was nice to have my lips locked on a pretty girl. But when I pulled back, looked behind her in hopes that Elle got the message and bothered some other poor fucker - Trinity had her naughty little mouth around, Darth-Vader Ben. It made me feel odd inside, jealous. I don't think I have seen her kiss someone else and it made me feel...sad.

What an odd feeling. I should be happy for my friend, right?

But I felt far from happy and because I thought Ben was a dickhole, it pissed me off more that she chose someone who I wanted to punch in the face. He was not right for her. When she pulled away from Ben, she looked straight at me. Instead of finding an afterglow of a kiss, all I saw in her eyes was hurt and it confused me even more. But I've had enough of all these feelings. I needed to leave and get my dick wet.

"Shall we get out of here?" I leaned down and whispered in her ear. She looked up at me, flashed a sweet smile, fluttered her eyelashes and nodded. I grabbed her hand, making our way to the exit, not looking back or telling the team we were off. I needed some space and some time to think.

"My hotel is only round the corner if you're interested?" I said as we entered the street.

"Oh, I'm interested." Great, because I had an itch to scratch, and she was the right person. As soon as we were in my hotel room, our clothes came off quickly. I didn't even bother to try and pleasure her first; I could feel how wet she was, eager too - which was even better. I covered myself and climbed onto the bed, planted soft kisses down her body and pushed myself into her warmth; oh, it felt good. I hadn't had sex in several days, and he was definitely getting upset with the lack of action.

That's probably why I had been feeling shit and funny about Trinity. I was just horny and needed to let off steam.

I fucked the girl hard; her high pitch moaning was a little annoying, but I needed the release. I came quickly, and she did, too. After, I felt great and much more relaxed. She wanted to cuddle and chat, which I really could not be bothered with; I wanted a shower and go to sleep. But we talked a little. I told her about the show, and she told me she was studying for her master's in Computer Science. She was smart and pretty, but my heart wasn't in it – it never was anymore. As soon as there was a lull in the conversation, I told her I was going for a shower. I washed the whole of the evening away. When I came out, I called her a taxi, and she left. She knew what this was: a quick hook-up and no promises.

I didn't even catch her name.

I lie awake most of the night, which frustrated the shit out of me. I finally dropped off around 5 a.m. into a restless sleep.

My phone buzzes me awake around midday, and it's my sister Nora – I have the joy of three of them, all older: Poppy, Gracie and Nora. Growing up was fun; they all fought like the day of reckoning, but they were always nice to me. I learnt a lot from them, maybe too much.

"What?" I answer grumpily.

"Well, hello to you, shitbag." I take it back; they're all horrible, and so was growing up with them. "Did I wake you up? It's lunchtime, you know?"

"Glad you can tell the time, Nora. What do you want?" I snark.

"Well, Mr. Happy," she proudly continues, " I know how much you love us all and how it's so bloody hard to get us all together. So I rang Pops and Gee Gee, and for some miraculous reason, we are all free next week for the Bristol show, so I bought tickets and we are going to come and see your fat ugly face!" I can practically hear her beaming; it's true our get-togethers are so infrequent nowadays, so this is nice news to hear.

"That's great," my tone softens.

"Urgh, sound a little happier," she quips.

"I've just woken up; this is the best I've got," I admit.

"How's the show going, little bro?"

"Yeah, good, really good, actually," I hear her husband shouting in the background.

"Gotta go, but I'll book us all somewhere for drinks after the show; see if we can do a late dinner or something,"

"Sounds great," I agree.

"Love your face." And with that, she disconnects the call.

The Christmas Market - Adam

ANDY WILLIAMS – IT'S THE MOST WONDERFUL TIME OF THE YEAR

I finally crawl out of bed just before dinner. I order room service from the restaurant downstairs and decide to continue writing and playing some music that I've been working on. Over the years, I have had quite a bit of music bought from me for adverts, low-budget movies and a few songs I've co-wrote that haven't quite hit the top ten, but they've been well-known within the charts. I love writing or playing music, but only on a low-key basis. I was never one for the limelight; my privacy is really important to me. I have seen many friends go into the limelight and have huge success but, are always torn apart and invaded by the media and I was never one for that route.

Still, for me, I was the support network, the background artist, and it paid my bills well. I know I could have hit the big time - if I had tried hard enough. I've even been offered a few contracts in my time, but I have always turned it down. I like my life busy if I want it to be, quiet if I want it to be. I like to buy my weekly shop at the supermarket looking like an absolute shit state knowing no one will bat an eyelid because, really, I'm a nobody - and my face won't be plastered in the papers or my name slandered all-over social media.

No fucking thanks.

When the hotel room starts to darken, I know I have been cooped up too long, so I head back out into the centre to check out the Christmas Market in the square, the gothic lions by the council house are a great touch to the city centre. I saw it last night on the way to the bar, making a mental note to visit. I want to buy some of the trinkets and worldly goods they sell for Christmas presents; my sisters love all that crap. The evening air is cold as I watch my breath swirl around my face - I'm glad I took my coat, scarf and hat.

I wander around the stalls and get invested in the Christmas spirit. About halfway around, I spot a bar that is serving mulled wine and German hotdogs. The smells are too good to ignore, and my stomach gurgles loudly – I'm not one to ignore the boss, so I queue up. As I'm reaching the front, I spot Trinity out of the corner of my eye; she catches mine, too, and for a second, I almost see her debate about coming over. But I give her my best smile, a wave and beckon her over. She's on her own and must be doing the rounds of the market, too.

"Hey stranger," she smiles at me, that sad smile again, "you, okay?"

"Yeah, still nursing a hangover," she looks a little sheepish, and I laugh. I'm served quickly, order two hot dogs and mulled wine, pay and hand one over to Trinity.

"Oh gosh, no, I can't," she holds her stomach, and for a moment, I think she may vomit.

"The hair of the dog and a massive sausage will make you feel better," her cheeks are red from the cold, but I see them redden further. I love flirty penis innuendoes! She takes it from me and starts to eat. I do the same, the mustard and spices make the food explode in my mouth. "Are you looking around the market?" she nods and we continue walking around the market together whilst finishing off our food. Trinity looks like she has a lot on her mind, and I'm not one to push. Having spent a lot of time with her at university, I know she'll talk when she's ready. I purchase a few more little bits for my sisters, and we enjoy the Christmas carols blasting out and the winter cheer. I spot the outdoor ice skating.

"I've always wanted to go ice skating outdoors," she admits with a spark in her eye.

"Let's do it then," I take her hand and pull her over to the kiosk. The rink doesn't look too busy. They have old-school Christmas songs belting out, with a Christmas tree in the middle of the rink, the twinkly lights are draped all over, and it's nice.

"No, Adam, no, I don't think skating on my hangover would do me good. Plus, I haven't skated in years," her protest will not work on me, we are doing this!

"All I'm hearing is excuses. It's Christmas Trin. Didn't you say you wanted new experiences? Plus, this is my Christmas wish for us, and you can't be all Scrooge and deny me my Christmas wish?" I pout for extra effect as she searches my face with a scowl.

"This is not your Christmas wish, Adam," she complains.

"How do you know you haven't even asked me?" I pay for two tickets before she can protest further, and quickly take off her shoes and lace her skates up.

"I can do it myself," she whines, folding her arms over her chest and it only makes her boobs look bigger.

Nice. Stop looking at your mate's boobs, Adam!

"I'm only being a gentleman to the lady," I joke; she gets up from the bench and almost falls on me. I catch her with ease as she lets out a little squeal. My dick perks up and the whole thing has me feeling odd. As soon as she is steady, I let go immediately, trying to put space between us.

Do I have feelings for Trinity?

I feel weird asking myself the question because she's always been my friend, but these last few days have brought back so many happy memories of her and me together, not of Cora. In fact, I haven't thought about her all week...since the tour began; I mean, it could be a coincidence and that I have been super busy, but...I let the thought linger for a moment.

"You okay in there, big boy?" Trinity muses, "Told you I was too much to handle with skates. You can back out now, I won't be offended. But, I will warn you that I will spend most of my time on the floor," I bark out a laugh and take her hand in mine.

"Never, we will rule the rink with our awesome skating skills," we go onto the ice and within seconds, we are both flying all over the place, landing on the icy floor, side-by-side laughing.

"Don't tell me you're crap at skating? Adam not good at something, shock, horror!" she opens her mouth wide and places her hand over it in pretend shock.

Before I can stop myself, I blurt, "Be careful how wide you open your mouth Trin, I might just stick my dick in there."

Trinity bursts into laughter, but as I said it, I don't think I'm joking; if her mouth is that big, how far could I stick him back there, like all the way back, deep-throating her dirty mouth?

What the hell is wrong with me?

She gets up clumsily and holds her hand out for mine. I pull myself up, careful not to pull her down again, and we make our way slowly, at first, around the ice. After a few minutes, we seem to have got a good rhythm going, and I start gaining confidence and doing a few turns and stops. Then my favourite Christmas song comes on, 'O Holy Night'. I love this song; this makes it Christmas in our house, Mum and Dad making the Christmas dinner, the shit ton of presents, the whole family together and a lot of laughter.

"I love this song," Trinity says with a smile on her face, "this reminds me of Christmas day when I was growing up; it always gives me the warm Christmas feels," her eyes are bright again and she's looking at me like I'm the best thing, spreading a tingling warmth across my body,

"No way, me too," she laughs, I laugh as well, and then it's silent, just staring at one another and I have never noticed how blue her eyes are. I don't quite get it, but we are definitely having a moment; a warmth spreads around my body, and it's not the mulled wine as I only had one. She looks away, clears her throat and checks her watch.

"I think I'm going to head back to the hotel. I want to get an early night as we are heading out pretty early tomorrow," she doesn't wait for my response, as if she feels uncomfortable too. Is she feeling this warmth too, or is it more of a stay away, you make me uncomfortable?

What the hell is going on?

The kiss - Trinity

IDINA MENZAL – BABY IT'S COLD OUTSIDE

I have to take a long, long shower after the evening I have had with Adam. His flirty banter was never amiss at university, but now it just feels like a slap in the face with a wet fish because he still loves Cora, because he left with someone else last night and today, he said NOTHING about it. It's not any of my business, I get that, but he didn't even say, 'Soz I left without saying bye last night' or, 'How was your night?' or even, 'Sorry I didn't kiss you last night'.

Then he was looking at me like he wanted to kiss me at the ice rink; he gave me 'the look,' the one where the eyes go a little glazed over. He flicked his eyes to my lips, and I swear I didn't imagine it, but he leant in a little - unless there was a planet shift and we were all leaning a little. I feel so confused, and this stupid shower isn't helping.

After the shower, I put on my pyjamas, take off my make-up and braid my hair to the side. Sitting on the bed, I start to wrap up some of the presents that I purchased from the Christmas market. The last posting date is in a few days, so I need to get this sorted quickly as who knows when I will have time to nip to a post office.

I realise halfway through that I have left one of the presents with Adam, as he offered to carry some of my bags. I internally curse myself, grab my key card and head off down the hall to his room. I linger outside his door for a moment and think it may be better to grab it off him tomorrow before we get onto the bus, but knowing him, he will be MIA, and I will be pissed if I miss the last post. I knock lightly on the door, and oh my shit, I'm not expecting him to answer the door in low sweatpants. His chiselled chest flirting in my face, and he has his glasses on – his beautiful Superman glasses. Honestly, I nearly have to pick myself up off the floor. He leans against the doorframe, showing off his perfect pecs, and his mouth twitches a little.

"Nice Pyjamas, Trin; also, my eyes are not on my chest," he playfully says.

I snap my eyes back to his, swallowing hard at this man of perfection. "Don't diss Winnie the Pooh," I ignore his other comment - I love Pooh Bear; my pyjamas are awesome, comfy and cool. He shrugs indifferently.

"It's cute," he remarks.

"Can you put a top on? It's really distracting," I ask.

"You came to my room, so my rules, no tops, so you know if you want to come in, top off," he winks at me. I roll my eyes, pretending that I'm not secretly excited that he wants to see me topless. Then I remember it's Adam, playboy douchebag. Nevertheless, the urge to run back to my room and touch myself, thinking of this moment of how beautiful he is, is not lost on me. He walks from the door, and I enter his room. He gets back on the bed cross-legged and pulls his guitar back to him. There are a lot of papers over his bed; he's in his writing mode. "What's up?" he scribbles on some of the paper, tucks his pencil behind his ear, and strums some notes on his guitar.

"I left one of my bags with you," he points to the chair, and I grab it. "What you working on?"

"Something and nothing," he remarks without looking up.

"Let's hear it then," I perch on the edge of the bed and read some of what he's written and the notes he's planned. I look up, and he seems shy at my request.

"I don't like to play anything that's unfinished," he admits. He runs his hand through his shaggy blonde hair.

"It's me; we used to play together all the time," he smirks at my remark, and I huff out an unimpressed look. I don't want to get sucked into his 'flirtiness'; it sends off all kinds of wrong messages to my brain - this is why it's taking me so long to get over him.

"That was different because we had no choice," he mutters.

I put my hand to my heart, "Ouch, I'm totally offended," he blows out a breath, and his cool blue eyes stare at me for a moment. I really did miss him in his glasses; he totally looks sexier in them.

"Okay," he whispers; I smile at him and sit cross-legged opposite him - he starts strumming. He plays the usual five chords, G major, C, E minor, A chord and D chord, but then he puts his style on it; I take a look at the words again.

"Are these the words?" I ask. He smiles sheepishly and nods; I take a look and really feel the music flow through me, and I start to hum along with the tune, then sing what he's written. I'm not the best singer, but I do alright for myself.

I have to let you go; even now, my heart says so.

I see you with him; my brain stops working like my breath.

It should have been me; it should have been me, but it's not.

It should have been us; you should have given me a shot.

I have to let you go. Even now, my heart says so.

I stop singing as he has stops playing; I snap my eyes up at him, confused, "Why did you stop?" he leans forward and kisses me. My heart soars; his kiss is powerful but gentle. He puts his hand on my neck and pulls me forward and I kiss him back. Just for a moment, I kiss him back, touching his soft lips. I have played this kiss out so many times before in my head. I think that it's the best kiss of my life until it's not. I pull back, I'm pissed.

"What are you doing?" I demand, slightly flustered.

"Kissing you, what does it look like?" I frown, trying to understand what is going on. I see a lot of emotions cover his face. I lean away and get off the bed. Sighing, I pace the room for a moment.

"I'm going to go," I grab my bag from the floor, I want to cry; my body is shaking and I'm cross.

"Was it that bad?" he jokes as he searches my face, "I'm sorry, it was a mistake; I won't do it again."

"Adam..." I whisper.

Does he not realise how deep this runs for me?

"I got caught up in the moment, you know, writing and singing music is my orgasm high, I thought...I don't know what I thought."

"Stop, please, just stop," I ask.

"I don't understand what's happening here, Trinity; you look so upset," I hear the hurt in his voice as he is trying to understand this situation as well.

"I am upset, don't you see?"

I have wanted this kiss for many years, all be it brief, but I won't be second to Cora, my best friend. Adam has been carrying a torch for her for years. He never looked twice at me when she was around. Even though Cora married Zach four months ago, I can see he is hurting still, fucking hell I just sang a song that is definitely about Cora. He stands up from the bed, puts his guitar down and envelopes me into a hug. He pulls back, and then he guides my face to look at him.

"Look, I'm sorry, Trinity, if I crossed the line. I wasn't thinking, but even I can see that you're upset about something more. I know I'm not that bad at kissing," I smile a little. "What's going on?"

There he is, there's the Adam that I remember. Sweet, thoughtful, kind and staring into his eyes, I see the man I fell in love with. My anger lessens to know he is in there somewhere. Not this 'gives no shit; treat women like they're crap' guy. He strokes my hair tenderly, and I notice all the little freckles on his nose.

Before I know it, my lips are on his, I feel his hand thread through my hair and groan into my mouth, and oh my shit, this is even more perfect. His tongue swipes into my mouth and I open greedily for him because all I ever wanted is him; all I ever saw is him, and here we are kissing. Not a peck, but full-on tongue, lips and moans. The last kiss was definitely a warm-up because this is off-the-charts panty-wetting stuff.

But he loves Cora.

I push him back, even angrier than before; I feel it vibrating through me now.

"I won't be your pity kiss," I blurt out. He furrows his eyebrows and looks at me, confused.

"Who said I pity you?" Even when he is confused or has his angry face on, he's still perfect.

"Not me, idiot, you, your pity kiss," I spit out.

"For who?"

"For Cora, who I know you have been in love with since day one," I declare. I don't mean it to come out so venomous or blunt, but I said it: what has been clinging onto me for years.

"Oh," he looks away, sad and hurt by my words, but I had to say it – didn't I? I promised myself that when I met someone, I would walk into a room, their eyes would light up and my eyes would always gravitate towards them. I wanted to be their one. I was never going to be Adam's one.

"You know she's pregnant?" I couldn't stop myself; the words tumble out like verbal poop. I want to hurt him, but really, I am only hurting myself. This kiss should never have happened. He looks at me like he wants to cry, and there it is, there is the confirmation I need that he and I will never work. No matter how badly I want him, I can never live up to Cora's standards in his eyes.

"No, I didn't know," he murmurs. He walks towards the window and looks out onto the city skyline. Someone had to rip the plaster off, and deliver the news – I'm glad it is me, a friend. However, I could have probably said it a bit nicer.

The room is silent and feels awkward as hell. I'm grateful that I don't bubble over and laugh at the awkwardness to relieve the tension. Instead, I walk over to the window and wrap my arms around him, resting my head on his back, loving his smell of freshly pressed washing and a hint of man. He smells beautiful. His arms lay limp for a moment and then he turns and holds me back.

"Thank you for telling me," he kisses me gently on the hair, and we hold each other in silence for a moment. "I think you should go." I nod, as the hurt creeps further into my heart and I scuffle out of his room, crawl into my bed and cry myself to sleep.

I will never be second best to anyone, no matter how much I love them.

Adam - Sadness

KT Tunstall – Lonely This Christmas

Once Trinity leaves the room, I face plant on the bed, screaming into the pillow in frustration. My glasses crush against my face, I pull them off and throw them across the room like a naughty child. How did Trinity know how I felt about Cora? Was I that transparent? Did everyone know how I felt about her, except her?

She's pregnant now too, the words I dreaded to hear. It hurt to know this, but not as much as I thought it would, which is a genuine relief. I don't think I could take that crushed feeling again. I feel like I'm only starting to recover from the fact that she married him. I mean, I'm not stupid, I know what comes after marriage; I thought I had more time before she decided to make babies.

She's pregnant.

I feel weirdly okay with that.

I now know that I never stood a chance. I realised that too late. I wasted all that time trying to be the nice guy, trying to be her friend and hoping that one day she would be mine, that she would wake up and know she belonged to me. That was the dream, but a dream is all it will ever be.

I lie on my back and look up at the ceiling. I knew my feelings for Cora had dialled back a notch; the pain, which had been too hard to breathe only a few months ago was now a dull ache. To be fair, in those few months I have drunk far too much and fucked through so many women - but it felt good not to give a shit. I have blocked Cora's number, and blocked all of her from my mind. I never wanted to look at her or speak to her again. She tried to text and call at first, but I was done with her. I have put as much distance as I could between her and me, which is a good thing. It felt better, a fresh start.

Cora will never be mine.

I say it over and over until I hope my brain and heart decide to understand and work together because I am tired of feeling like this.

I roll onto my side and think of Trinity. I got so caught up in the moment, without thinking, I leaned forward and kissed her. The way she lights up when she is singing, listening or playing music makes me want to be near her and all the energy she gives off. The way we were together as I played and she sang my song - it was mesmerising. It wasn't something I had felt before, it was intimate and beautiful, and I liked that feeling very much. It was like being back at university, the good old times and I missed it. I missed Trinity, her friendship, her kindness, just her. And then I kissed her and now I've frigging ruined it, I was so lost in the moment, lost in her.

But why did I kiss her?

She was so angry at me, and I couldn't figure out why. It was only a kiss.

Wasn't it?

The thoughts roll around my head, and I fall into a restless sleep. The next morning, we drive down to Cardiff. I'm super glad that I'm in the car with Elijah because I need to stay away from Trinity. I have to gain some perspective. I liked kissing her, she's fiery and passionate, but I have upset her. I wanted to be there for her, to be a good person, but I wasn't even sure who I was anymore. I didn't want to lose Trin as well; her friendship was too important.

Elijah gives me shit about being quiet and coaxes some of the story out of me, even though I didn't want to talk about it. He listens, which is one of the things I like about our friendship. We could be ridiculous when we want to be, but we also are patient with one another. When I finish my verbal diarrhoea on the situation, he gives me a shit-eating grin.

"What?" I ask, confused.

"You like her!" I shake my head and scoff, "You do; you're fucking finally over, Cora, which I'm not going to lie is the saddest tale of my life and now you've grown up, I'm so proud of you!"

"I don't like her, not like that," I admit.

"Sure, you don't," he responds sarcastically. Elijah's phone rings and it's the theatre calling asking for an ETA and to go over the schedule. So, I let his words settle in my mind.

Do I like her?

As we sat down to play that evening in the Orchestra pit, I realised I hadn't spoken to her all day. We smile in passing but nothing else, she has been avoiding me, too. I guess we both don't really know what to say. During the show, I couldn't help but sneak a look (or two) at Trinity. I couldn't help but watch her play, the little crease in her forehead, the way she bites her lip in concentration and when she closes her eyes and loses herself to the music, she really is breathtaking to look at – just like last night.

How had I never seen this before?

Because all I ever saw was Cora. All my thoughts for years have been about her. I curse myself again about my stupid infatuation with Cora. I think I need to have an honest conversation with myself and then another one with Trinity about what this is between us. I feel different; this whole thing between me and Trinity has shifted, and it's nothing like how I felt with Cora; this was something stronger, something real.

Does she feel the same way?

No, this is ridiculous; I don't do relationships remember? It is a fleeting moment between two fantastic musicians doing what we love to do. I was caught up in the moment, but fuck, what a great moment it was. Imagine if we hadn't stopped kissing. I bet sex with Trinity is wild, and with that thought, I'm straining against my boxers and all I can think about is sliding my dick into Trinity. Thank goodness the guitar is over my crotch as this would be a bit embarrassing.

When the show ends, I decide that I'm going to ask Trin for a drink, just me and her and have a talk. As we pack up, I see Ben and Trinity talking and laughing, she doesn't even look at me, and that hurts - a lot more than I thought.

Why won't she look at me? Maybe she's so hurt that I pushed the boundaries last night; she doesn't want to talk to me anymore, and she doesn't like me that way.

Fuck, stop procrastinating and talk to her!

I pack my guitar away and head out to the bus to store it for the journey. As I come back round to the side, I stop in my tracks, and that's when I see them. My stomach does that twisty, funny turn like it used to when I saw Cora and Zach together, the hurt and the longing. But it's not Cora; it's Trinity and Ben, kissing in the shadows of the building. A deep, passionate one; he has pulled her close, and her arm is hooked around his neck. He has one hand around her waist and the other on her cheek, and there's tongue, definitely tongue, but I can't look away. I stare for longer than I should.

"They look cute together, don't they?" Elle chimes in as she walks past with her violin. I look at her nodding, but really all I want to do is go down into the shadows and punch his face in because he got Trinity, not me.

Did I really mean nothing? Is that what I am to her?

Trinity – Another City

WHAM – LAST CHRISTMAS

We have driven to Cheltenham today. I love travelling, and for once in England, it's starting to snow, only a small flurry, but that's got everyone excited, the roads are almost at a standstill and everyone is on high alert. With just over seven days until Christmas, I am feeling super Christmassy. I posted all my cards and presents, and now I feel I can relax because guess what? It's Christmas. I love the build-up, the cold weather and my breath swirling around in the cold. I love warm fires, hot chocolate, mulled wine, the trees, lights, the smells, just all of it. Call me Mrs. Klaus because I would happily marry Santa and be an all-year-round Christmas lover!

It's been three days since the passionate kiss with Adam, yet we've barely spoken, Adam is still being quiet, he isn't avoiding me as such, but he isn't being his usual chatty self. I know he thinks the kiss was a mistake. I replay the words he said to me in my head: 'I'm sorry, it was a mistake, I won't do it again.'

Then, when I told him about Cora being pregnant, his features said it all and that crestfallen face is also what replays in my head over and over again. He doesn't want me, he will never want me, but that kiss will always remain seared in my brain. It was amazing, definitely one of the best kisses I have ever had – that thought makes me sad that I won't experience that with him again. But, I have to be okay with that because this tour was about moving on with my life, and that's what I intend to do. I feel proud of myself that I don't want to run and hide or wallow in self-pity - that makes me feel happier and stronger that I'm willing to find love again – just not with Adam.

Ben was relentless, he cornered me after the show in Cardiff and I felt so sad about Adam. So, I did the worst thing: I kissed Ben to make myself feel better. He told me all the things I wanted to hear, how beautiful I was and how much he liked me and the next thing I knew, we were kissing. In comparison to the fireworks and panty-wetting kiss of Adam, Ben was a sparkler. I wanted it to be enough, but after that kiss with Adam, I knew Ben wasn't right for me. Despite how lovely it was and I did like him, I didn't feel the connection or the chemistry. When we are all out tonight, I will pull him to one side and tell him I want to be friends. I don't want to string him along; he isn't what I'm looking for. I'm a true romantic. Also, I have watched too many romantic films, they've ruined my perception of the perfect relationship and now I want the whole package: the fireworks when kissing, the explosive orgasms and to be treated as if I'm the only person in the world who exists. I think I have too high of an expectation, but I will find him – he has to be out there somewhere.

Cheltenham was a fantastic evening; the Regency buildings are awe-in-spiring and another beautiful place to perform in - we even played a few carols - the audience sang along; it was so much fun. It's got me on a Christmas high and I can't wait to go out and dance tonight. We have a later start tomorrow, a sort of morning off, as Elijah wants to head down to Bristol instead of staying here for two nights. Either way, I love the Cheltenham nightlife and everyone wants to party tonight. The snow lasted all of two hours and didn't settle, to my disgust, but the bitter nights are here to stay, but that won't dampen my spirits. I've dressed in skinny jeans and a tight sparkly top; my teal heals, curled my hair and have gone a bit garish with my green make-up and hooped earrings; I look good and feel good. We all ate at the hotel restaurant but it seemed Adam didn't want to join us, to my disappointment, but the rest of the group were on form, so I pushed the feeling aside and with only four more shows to play, everyone was in the mood to party.

We head out and find a great club called 21, the music is R&B and I love the bass sounds that skitter across the floor and vibrate through my body. Ben is being quite touchy-feely in the club and I pull him to the outside smoking area for a chat as soon as possible; it's secluded and not many people are out there, so it's a good place to talk. He pulls me into a hug, which I awkwardly hug back, and then he goes to kiss me - but I pull away.

"Is something wrong?" his eyes are a bit unfocused, so I know he has been drinking.

Shit, I really should have spoken to him earlier.

But I kept chickening out as confrontation is never my thing. I hate hurting people's feelings.

"No, Ben, erm, the thing is," he tries to kiss me again. I step back, trying to put some space between us.

"What?" he raises his hands in confusion.

"I think we should be friends," I look him in the eye and say it with as much confidence as possible.

"Okay," he smiles and cuddles into me and kisses me on the neck. I stand back again.

"Ben, did you hear me?" I ask.

"Yes, I heard you. You want to be friends." I smile, glad that he under-stands. He goes to kiss me again.

"Ben, what are you doing?" I try to keep the tension out of my voice, but I hate it when people don't respect my boundaries.

"Friends kiss...and fuck," he smiles.

"I don't think they do, not like this. I'm saying I don't want a relationship with you."

"Who said anything about a relationship, Trinity? I only wanted to make out and get you into my bed; it wasn't ever going to be a long-term thing," he licks his lips.

"You're drunk!" I declare.

"Yes, but sober or drunk, I still want to fuck you," he announces. This is crass. I mean, I get his honesty, but it hurt. I thought we were developing something before Adam came and ruined it with his tongue thrusts in my mouth.

"Yes, well, I don't want that." He shrugs as if my words mean nothing.

"Shame, I think you and I would have had some wild nights together," he then spots Elle and walks off to talk to her. I stand there a little in shock.

What the hell just happened? Well, his words and actions just made me feel like crap.

My phone buzzes and I take it from my bag. Mum has texted to say she has got tickets to the Bournemouth show, and I inwardly groan. Can this evening get any worse? I look up from giving Mum a thumbs-up text, to Ben kissing Elle.

Nope, there it is, it just got worse

The call - Adam

SIA - UNDER THE MISTLETOE

I didn't go out last night. I wasn't feeling it; not even the thrill of a hook-up got me fired up; I felt weird. Maybe I was coming down with the flu. I got up early this morning and pounded out some frustration in the hotel gym and then ate an early breakfast. My phone rings as I am packing my bags to leave for the next city. I feel so much better after a very long shower and a wank. It's Charlie. He has called me a few times, and I feel bad that I'd forgotten to call him back.

"Hey mate, how's the tour going? The London ladies are missing you!" I chuckle.

"It's going well, much better than I thought it would be," I admit.

"Yes, that's because you're getting a variety of pussy every night!" I laugh at his dirty humour but don't follow up on his remark. "Oh gosh, are you in a dry spell?"

"No, nothing like that," I say.

"Well, spit it out, mate. I've got rehearsal in ten, and I can't figure out the undertone of this conversation. What's happening on tour? Oh man, did you and Elijah suddenly make out? I always thought you had some man chemistry going on," the humour in his tone doesn't go amiss.

"What? No, no, nothing like that, it's nothing, just...Trinity is here," I confess quietly.

"Trinity Kirby from university?" Charlie asks.

"Yeah, weird, right?" I pointed out.

"No way, I haven't seen Trinity in ages. Is she still fit?"

"What?" I ask, confused. When did he notice that?

"Oh, come on, she was so fit at university. Have you banged her?"

"No!" I protest.

"Ah, man, I would have so banged her by now. I asked her at university, but she said no," he sounded sad about this, and I wondered if we even went to the same university; it seems I missed out on so much stuff whilst I was there.

"Wait, what?"

"Yeah, bummer, she looked like she'd be great in bed," he sighs as if he has missed the best opportunity with her.

"I think I like her...?" I admit and then ask it as a question as well; I'm so confused. Charlie barks a laugh down the phone.

"Finally, you know she's been in love with you forever," he declared.

That's a lot of pressure.

"What? Was she? Is she? Fuck off," my stomach starts to bubble with excitement, Trinity is in love with me?

"She looked at you the way that you looked at Cora. You just never saw it; I don't understand why you didn't close that chapter on Cora ages ago. Trinity is well-fit, and I would have shagged her ages ago. I mean, I can't say if she likes you now as you're a mess, and even I know not to go near a cannonball of an explosion like you. So, she probably hates you now."

"Yeah, that sounds more like it. She kissed someone else," I mumble because saying that out loud hurts.

"So? It's just a kiss. They're not together, right? She's not getting married?" I groan at his playful tone. "Just do me a favour and fuck her for me. I think I lost out big time with her. So anyway, what are you getting me for Christmas?"

"Nothing, I will be home; we can get drunk, same old, same old," I joke.

"Nah mate, I'm going away this Christmas, so get me a present, something nice, yeah? Anyway, gotta run, see you at New Year."

Sometimes my best friend is a nob!

~

We arrived in Bristol just before lunch. As we drove down, Elijah mentioned Trinity was unwell and asked if I knew anything about it. I was surprised to hear this as much as he was. He studied me to see if I was telling the truth or if I had done something, but for once, it wasn't me. Elijah also said she'd caught the earlier train and was already in Bristol and checked in at the hotel. This was odd. I wondered what had happened to cause her to leave early as we hadn't spoken, so I was unsure if she was okay. I was half tempted to text her, but I didn't. It wasn't until we arrived at the hotel that I realised it might be to do with Elle and Ben locking lips like love-sick teenagers, and I couldn't help but smile. Ben the dickhead had come through; maybe he doesn't need a punch but a handshake for being such a douchebag. But if he had hurt Trinity, I was going to kill him. The possessiveness of making sure Trinity was okay seemed oddly overwhelming.

What was wrong with me?

I wanted to run to Trinity's room, but I stopped myself for two reasons. One, I still had no idea what I wanted to say, and two, when I turned up at the hotel, all three of my sisters were there. I had totally forgotten they were coming to the show.

"Surprise," they squeal as they hug me in the foyer of the hotel. It is a surprise, but I'm also annoyed that I can't go and figure this thing out with Trinity. I really did need to talk to her. Guess that's not going to happen.

"We've booked a restaurant for lunch just around the corner," Poppy declares happily. I check into my room at reception and dump my bags there. I will sort that out later. We leave to eat lunch because I'm starving, and I don't want to watch Elle and Ben dry-humping each other.

"I thought we were meeting tomorrow after the show?" I ask, confused because usually, I don't listen to half the stuff that comes out of their mouths, but I definitely knew they were watching the show tomorrow. They'd texted me daily to remind me.

"Well, an afternoon with our favourite brother was what we all needed instead," Gracie, my eldest sister, jokes.

"I'm your only brother, so I have to be your favourite," I declare.

"True, it was slim pickings. With work on Monday, we didn't want to stay out late, so we booked a hotel room here tonight, too! So, catch us up on everything."

The lunch turns into a very long catch-up, and before we know it, it's time to order dinner. Not that the restaurant owners are complaining, we have ordered a lot of food and drinks during the day. I'm about 6 pints in and thoroughly buzzed, but out of the corner of my eye, I see her. I think I could be absolutely slaughtered, and I would still find her. I can't help but jump out of my seat, almost knocking over my chair and race out of the restaurant.

"Trinity!" I shout as I catch up with her a few shops down. She turns around wearing a cute hat and warm coat, all bundled up with a red nose. She looks so beautiful. My voice gets caught in my throat because the urge to kiss her is overwhelming and catches me off guard. I never thought I would feel like this about anyone ever again, but here we are. It's exhilarating, and yet I'm terrified. I need to know how she feels about me, I can't go through this again; I can't lose her, too.

"Oh, hey Adam, I was just getting some fresh air before dinner," she frowns, "Are you okay? And why are you not wearing a coat? It's bloody freezing!"

"I'm having dinner with my sisters," I smile as I know how much she likes them. Whenever they came to visit me at university, we always went out for dinner together. They got on so well, usually putting the world to rights or ganging up on me.

"No way, they're all here?" I nod with a big smile because I know she'll want to see them. I also know that means we will spend the evening together and now she can't avoid me. Right now, I love my sisters being here.

"Come say hi," I coax. Her eyes light up. She links her arm with mine, and now everything feels right with the world again.

The dinner - Trinity

KELLY CLARKSON – WRAPPED IN RED

As I entered the restaurant, I was glad of the warmth, as I had been walking around the block for a good twenty minutes. I was unsure what to eat and still processing my feelings about...well, everything. I left early on the train this morning; I wanted space after what had happened between me and Ben last night. Not because I was upset that he literally licked Elle's face off in front of me or, that they went back to the hotel together and most likely had sex. It was because it hurt that he had cast me aside so easily after I said no to having sex with him. I thought we had forged a nice friendship or something.

Was I that gullible? Was sex the only thing he wanted from me? Was it that I always saw the best in people? All my thoughts were tiring and overwhelming, so a quiet ride on the train was a must. I couldn't quite face the crowds of my team on the bus. I texted Elijah, faking a headache and said I would make my own way there so that he wouldn't worry.

I felt slightly relieved as well that I wasn't Ben's hook-up, especially if that was how quickly he dismissed me when he realised we wouldn't have sex. It made me feel icky inside, and so riding the bus with them this morning felt all kinds of wrong. Plus, when I bumped into Tom (the pianist) in the hotel corridor, he said he wished he had taken the train too, as they were literally making out all the way there, and even he felt like gagging – so I think I did myself a favour.

I arrived nice and early and went for a walk around Bristol. With the sea so close, it felt like a little holiday with the cold, fresh, salty air. I semi-wish it was summer so I could lie on the beach and inhale the vitamin D. Instead, there's an icy chill on the breeze and temperatures are lulling between -2 and -4. I then checked in, took a bath and napped. I called Cora when I woke up. It was so nice to catch up with her, but I didn't mention anything about Adam or the fact he was on tour with me. I wanted it to be my secret, even though saying that now sounds silly. We spoke about Ben and what a lucky escape I had and how she was going to try and come to the last show in London. I love how she always comes to one of my shows when I was playing, and I always did the same where possible. Her friendship and support have always been important to me.

But this time, I tried to put her off, telling her that it was fine if she couldn't make it and we would see each other at New Year. If she came, then she would see Adam, and I'm not sure how that would work. Cora would ask too many questions and try to talk to Adam, and what would Adam do? He would continue to show me how much he was in love with Cora and not me. I wasn't sure if anybody was ready for that meeting yet.

After we said our goodbyes, it was starting to get dark, and my tummy rumbled. I thought I would have a look at the Christmas lights in the town centre and then go in search of some food.

I get a little lost on the way back, but if I hadn't, then I wouldn't have seen Adam's sisters. I really like them; they're such a laugh. I order a large glass of red and we spend the next few hours catching up on life. It's so nice hearing about how they're married and pregnant and all the good things in life. They all seem really happy and settled. I order a pie, mashed potato with roast vegetables for my dinner. It's a proper winter warmer, and it's so nice.

When Adam goes to the toilet, all the girls look at me oddly, but I'm so stuffed from eating my weight in delicious food I don't notice at first - the food coma is taking over.

"What? Why are you looking at me like that?" They smile as if they just heard the best secret of their life.

"What's happening between you and Adam?" Nora asks, I look at them, confused. Poppy sighs with relief.

"Oh, I'm so glad you said it; you see it too, right?" They all nod.

"He literally lit up when he saw you walk by," Gracie confesses.

"I've never seen him move like that," Nora giggles.

"He won't stop looking at you like Christmas has come early," they all laugh and start chatting between themselves.

"No, no, it's not like that. He's never seen me like that," I declare.

"But you have?" Poppy asks. I turn a shade of red, and they all murmur in agreement.

"Not anymore," I whisper. Poppy holds my hand.

"What did he do? I'm not afraid to cut his dick off!" I laugh.

"Too far Poppy, too far," Nora adds.

"No, he hasn't done anything; he's just different. I just don't know any-more," I admit.

"Don't know what?" Adam asks as he sits back at the table.

"If you wash your hands after you go to the toilet," I quickly add, "the first show we did, he didn't wash his hands, and my estimation of his cleanliness has gone downhill." We all laugh as he shoves his hands in my face.

"Smell them, soap and all," I bat his hand away. Adam yawns, stretching his arms up, showing a little of his firm stomach and I look away, trying not to stare.

"Look, I love you sisters, but we need to head back; it's late, and we have to get up early in the morning for practice as it's a double show," they all groan.

"We are going to stay for one more, we never get together, and with Poppy birthing a beautiful baby in the New Year, we will not get this chance again for a while. So be free, brother," Nora declares, "and we shall see your lovely faces tomorrow."

I give them all hugs with promises I will come down to Devon at some point and see them next year. Adam helps me into my coat, and we exit the restaurant. The walk back to the hotel is in comfortable silence, and it feels like things have shifted again to business as usual. I'm glad as I felt worried that since that kiss, I might lose Adam as a friend.

When we enter the hotel foyer, Ben and Elle are there holding hands waiting for the lift. They look like they have been out for dinner too. I stop walking, not wanting them to see us, but Adam nudges me along. I veer towards the stairs, but Adam links his arm with mine and guides me to the lift.

The bastard.

The lift dings and we all get in together.

Well, this is bloody awkward.

Elle and Ben then realise that we are all in the lift together. Ben's whole demeanour changes; he then gives Adam a shit-eating grin.

"Do you have something to say?" Adam growls out at him.

"Nothing at all," he says with a smile on his face. Elle casts her eyes to the floor. I hate confrontation. Adam and Ben have a silent eye fight and I don't miss that Adam has also balled his fists up. The lift dings again to indicate my floor.

What is happening right now?

Adam and I get out of the lift and walk along the corridor.

"What was that?" I ask Adam as we stop outside my hotel room door.

"Nothing," he mumbles. I place my keycard on the door and it unlocks. I push it open slightly and turn back to Adam.

"Well, thank you for a lovely evening. I really do like your sisters, so thank you for inviting me." His cool blue eyes stare back at me as if wanting to say something more, but instead, he leans in and kisses me on the cheek. He then whispers in my ear.

"It was my pleasure," a warm shiver runs down my body. As he pulls back, he looks at me.

Oh, how he looks at me.

He has never looked at me like this before, like he wants to devour me. I swallow hard, unsure of what to say, unsure how to feel; my heart is beating so hard in my chest.

Are we going to kiss? Shall I kiss him?

I want to kiss him so much it hurts. I want him to want me like I want him. Before a rational decision in my head is made, Adam walks away, "Good night, Trinity," he husks out. I walk into my room and close my door, feeling slightly disappointed.

Holy shit, that is not business as usual; with all this sexual tension running through my body, I need a lie down with my vibrator – now!

Another show - Adam

Ava Max - Christmas Without You

Since Bristol, things have been better between me and Trinity, and after Ben's display of stupidity, the need to protect Trinity is high on my agenda and an inner struggle about why I am feeling this way. So, to satisfy my urge, I thought I would grace the bus with my presence, keeping Trinity nearby. I got a few whoops from the team and 'you've turned to the dark side' was also uttered when I sat down on the bus. But the real reason was to spend more time with Trinity.

It's only a few hours' drive down to Bournemouth and I have put on a film for us to watch. Trinity is biting her nails, a thing she used to do just before a big performance at university when she was anxious. I partly wondered if I pushed her a little too far the other night by making her come to dinner with my sisters, but I was selfish and so happy to see her walk by the restaurant.

Or it could be that I wanted to kiss her goodnight when I left Trinity at her hotel room; it took so much restraint and willpower to walk away. I was worried that she wouldn't want me to, and then we would go back to barely talking. But the main worry was that once I started, I wouldn't be able to stop. I pause the film halfway through and she's staring out the window and hasn't even noticed.

"What's up?" I ask. She pulls her thoughts from looking at the motorway traffic to the present.

"Huh?" I pull her fingers from her mouth and hold it in mine. She looks at my hand and then back at my face. "Did you say something?"

"Trin, you only bite your nails when you're worried. What's wrong?" she furrows her eyebrows at me and gets that cute little crease in her forehead, whisps of hair fall in front of her face and I squeeze her hand to encourage her to talk. But, also to stop myself from touching her further.

"My parents are coming to watch the show tonight," she blurts out. I almost sigh with relief that it's nothing to do with me.

"Ah, Mr and Mrs Kirby are gracing us with their presence, are they?" I chuckle, and she smiles. I know that the relationship with her parents is a little strained. I rub my thumb on her hand gently and she pulls her hand away. I was hoping the action would be a soothing contact, but it seems to agitate her further. "Do you want me to come with you? I could be your knight in shining armour?" I grin at her, trying to smooth the tension between us, but my rubbish joke goes down like a Brussels sprout serving at Christmas dinner. I seem to be doing a shit job. I search her face. "So?"

"So, what?" she asks, snapping her eyes back to meet my stare.

"Do you want me to come with you? I mean, you saved me from my sisters," I muse.

"Yeah, well, that wasn't really saving you; I had a great night. I can't ask you to sit through a tedious dinner with my parents," she mumbles.

"I want to," I say casually, but I do want to; I want to support her; she seems so anxious and that protective instinct washes over me like crazy. I grab her hand back and hold it tighter - this time, she doesn't refuse. We watch the rest of the movie as the rest of the crew are either napping or quietly talking on the bus. The drive down there isn't too bad, and the traffic is okay. I'm sad it hasn't taken longer so I can spend a bit more one-on-one time with Trinity. As we pull up to the hotel, my phone buzzes, and I see that Elijah has texted me:

'Don't fuck her until we finish the last set, I need my musicians in one piece until the end.'

I don't blame him for having this opinion, I've honestly lost count of how many women I've fucked these past several months, and I'm not proud of it. But he needn't worry; I didn't know what was even happening between us both

The Bournemouth show isn't half bad, and now there's only one last show to perform. I'm actually feeling sad it's the end of the tour. I notice Trinity's leg bouncing all the way through the show. She bites her plump lips even more so than usual, and I'm slightly ashamed that I feel aroused by her actions, but it's yet another sign she's nervous about seeing her parents. I want to hold her close and tell her everything will be fine. But she seems distant and cold this evening, and I don't want to upset her further. We only have an afternoon and early evening show today, which suits me fine as instead of finishing at almost midnight, we are done and dusted by 9 p.m.

Trinity wants to head back to the hotel and freshen up, so I decide to do that myself. I shower, spray on my aftershave, minus the shaving, and wear some nice trousers, shoes, a shirt and a tie. I've met Trinity's parents quite a few times, so they know me of a sort; they always seemed blunt but friendly. They were never around a lot, and I remember Trinity saying how much they disliked her taking music as a degree, but they never missed any of her shows.

I knock at Trinity's door just after half 9, knowing we have a 10 p.m. reservation. When she answers the door, I nearly jiz in my pants because she looks stunning. She's curled her hair, her make-up is subtle brown, and her dress is some sort of strapless curvy concoction and sparkles. I swallow hard at the thought of having to keep my hands to myself again, so I hide them in my pockets, discreetly adjusting my boxers.

"You look amazing," I whisper, trying not to choke on my own words. I've never seen Trin like this before, or maybe I have, but never noticed. I don't know; my brain is scrambled, and I can't think straight.

"Thanks," she gives me a little flirty twirl, "you look very handsome too, Adam," she sighs, "I really want to cancel."

"Cancel then. We can order takeout and watch a movie," she groans with another sigh. We both know she can't cancel. One thing I did know about her parents was cancelling is never an option, and neither is being late. "Come on then, Miss Kirby, let me take you out."

The parents - Trinity

KELLY CLARKSON – CHRISTMAS ISN'T CANCELLED (JUST YOU)

We arrive shortly after ten. The restaurant is still quite busy despite the late hour, and Adam is adamant the whole way in holding my hand. The reassurance helps, and I'm glad I don't have to face my parents alone – maybe with me having company, they'll be okay, but I wasn't betting on it. I don't think they even realise their passive-aggressive comments or their little put-downs that they reserve just for me. I have never seen them this way towards my brother, but he is the golden child, the one who did exactly what my parents wanted. So, is this my penance for following my dreams?

All I know is I'm going to walk away tonight feeling like a bag of shit and then spend weeks drowning in ice cream, trying to make myself feel better and having many 'mirror talks' to myself about how I'm not worthless.

The waiter shows us to the table, and I'm not sure if my parents are happy to see me as I haven't seen them since my birthday in the summer. Six months between us is not long enough, that's for sure. The frown on my dad's face and the tight smile on my mum's has my anxiety almost bubbling over. I take a quick, deep breath.

You can do this, Trinity!

"Mum, Dad, you remember Adam?" I force the biggest smile at them as I approach the table. The waiter pulls out the seat, and I'm grateful to sit down. I might pass out with my heart beating so fast and the weak feeling in my legs. We are here to fight, not flight, body; sort it out. I look at Adam, all relaxed and envy his outlook at this moment.

"Mr and Mrs Kirby, what a pleasure to see you again," he leans over the table and shakes Dad's hand. My mum gives him a tight, polite smile.

I almost laugh at how 'proper' he is towards my parents when I know how he really is, all full of swear words and sexual innuendos.

"You're late," my dad says. Not hello, how are you, or it's been too long we missed you, just late. My stomach knots, five seconds in, and he's on my case.

"Oh, that was me," Adam says whimsically, "I needed to go back and get changed. You know how it is when being in a big theatre show."

"Not really," my mum says. "How is your little show going?" she asks. Her tone has a hint of condescension at the word little, and I see Adam tense slightly. I wave at the waiter furiously and order a bottle of wine, to which my mother tuts, "Still drinking, I see." I don't bother to respond; it's not worth the arguments anymore. The thing is, I'm not a massive drinker. Just when my parents are around, I need it to help me through the ordeal.

"Mrs Kirby," Adam quips in, "the show is doing excellently; the reviews on social media and in the paper have raved about it, saying it's the best Christmas production the country has seen in years. What did you think?" I groan slightly, and Adam darts his eyes at me, not realising what a can of worms he has opened.

"We are not a big fan of the theatre," my dad answers, "I think it's a lot of nonsense, and when we come to watch Trinity in there, we don't get to see her anyway. Pointless."

Where is the waiter with my drink?

"But you can hear her, and she's fantastic," I love his enthusiasm, but the thought of banging my head on the table until I pass out seems like the only way out right now.

"Yes, she and everyone else playing music. How do we know which one she is?" Adam goes to open his mouth again, but I place my hand on his leg under the table and shake my head slightly, asking him to stop – which I am grateful he does. "I ordered dinner for us all."

At that moment, four steaks arrive at the table - I inwardly cringe. I hate steak; they know I hate steak, and Adam is a vegetarian. The waiter sets down the wine and I pour a very large glass and take several large gulps, to which my mum then sighs again. I notice Adam look down, horrified at the food placed in front of him. I slip my hands in his and squeeze them tight, but I think this time he isn't going to hold back.

"I appreciate you ordering, Mr. Kirby, but I'm a vegetarian." My Dad stops chewing his food and looks completely bewildered. "I don't eat meat."

"Who doesn't eat meat? What a ridiculous notion; everyone eats meat," he cuts up his steak angrily and shoves another piece in his mouth.

"No, actually they don't. It's actually really bad for the environment; even the government has an initiative to help people cut down their meat intake, and being a vegetarian means fewer animals are killed-" he snorts.

"Can you believe all this tripe, Carol?" my dad asks Mum. My mum nods in agreement, "I never asked for a lecture on what being a vegetarian is; now, eat up. It's rude not to clear a plate."

"So, how are you both?" I ask, trying to sound positive but mainly trying to steer this conversation in a different way.

"We are both well; we are still sad that you are not coming for Christmas day this year," Adam raised an eyebrow at me with this information.

"We haven't seen you in so long. Maybe if you got a steady job like your brother, then we would see you more often."

Oh no, not this!

"You know," Dad chimes in, "Will was saying they had an opening at his company in a more junior role. You'd have to go back and study a proper degree, but I said we should put your name forward. You could work your way up, get into the proper working environment, make some money." I can feel Adam actually vibrating in anger. I take another large gulp of wine and push my food around my plate. My dad doesn't even realise how he insults and hurts me with remarks like this.

"I told you, Dad-" I start.

"Yes, you did," he continues dismissively, "but I still think this job will be better. It's time to put a stop to all this music nonsense and get a proper job. Isn't that right, Carol?" Mum nods in agreement again whilst politely cutting her steak into small pieces and chewing delicately. Her whole demeanour is small and delicate. With not a hair out of place and make-up perfected. Yes, her lines have deepened with age, but her strict essence has always been you have to look and act perfectly – drawing attention to yourself is not ladylike.

"So let me get this right," Adam almost spits out. He's struggling to hide the anger in his voice and right now, I want the ground to swallow me up. Maybe facing this alone would have been a better idea. "You think that Trinity should get a corporate job because you don't believe in the arts?" his laugh is hysterical, "That is the stupidest thing I have ever heard. Do you not realise how talented your daughter is?"

"Is it really talent, though? It doesn't pay the bills, the flat she lives in is small, and she's more out of a job than in one. So clearly, she's not good enough to make it full-time; it's reality," my dad says mat-ter-of-factly, and I shrink into my chair with the scrutiny he gives me.

"I'm not staying for this shit. I can't believe you cannot see how wonderful and musically talented Trinity is," he stands from his chair, his voice even but full of venom, "she's one of the best violinists I know and have seen in a long time. The fact you can't love and support her just as she is makes me sick to my stomach – and not because you stuck meat on my plate," he looks down at me. "I'm sorry, Trinity," and he storms out of the restaurant.

Tears pool in my eyes. He stood up for me. No one has ever done that for me before. A warmth spreads around my body.

"What a horrible man," my mum adds. I push back my chair.

"Actually, you are both the horrible ones," I mutter.

"Young lady-" Dad interrupts.

"No, no, I can't do this anymore. Have a lovely Christmas." With that, I leave the restaurant. I know it doesn't sound much, but that is the first time I have ever spoken back to my parents, and it feels good.

Really good.

The dinner - Adam

ELLA HENDERSON – BLAME IT ON THE MISTLETOE

I storm out of the restaurant. I've never felt so protective of anyone before, well, apart from my sisters, but they could always hold their own. The way that Trinity was letting them talk to her like that made my blood boil and my skin crawl. She is amazing and talented and *everything*. But her parents couldn't see it, and Trinity sat there and said nothing.

Why?

I stomped along the street, full of anger; I couldn't sit with them for another second. I am back at the hotel within minutes, taking the stairs two at a time. I enter the hotel room and pace. I knew why I was feeling like this; oh shit, I like her; I like her a lot more than I realised. I couldn't lie to myself anymore. I sit down on the edge of my bed, trying to calm my feelings, to calm my heart and mind.

There's a small knock at my door. I open it up, and Trinity is standing there, her head and eyes cast down. She slowly raises her eyes and looks at me. I can tell she has been crying and that she's hurting. I pull her into a hug, kicking the door closed and just hold her. She shakes with silent cries for a few moments. I kiss her on the top of her hair softly and sniff her floral scent. I pull back and smooth away her tears with the tips of my fingers.

"Thank you," she whispers and looks at me with her glassy eyes. I hate seeing her sad.

"For what?" I stroke her hair back and push the stray tears with the pad of my thumb.

"For coming with me, for sticking up for me, for being there for me. No one has done that before." I stroke her cheek as she leans into my touch.

"Trin, I don't know why you let them talk to you like that," I try to say with more venom in my voice than I intend.

"It's complicated," she admits sadly.

"You know you are not any of those things, right? You are smart, talented, beautiful and it makes me so frustrated that they don't see any of that in you because you are all of that and so much more." She gives me a sad smile, and I think fuck it, it might as well all come out. "You are the most beautiful and strongest woman I know," I hear her breath catch as I lean towards her.

"Adam," she whispers, and then we kiss, soft and gentle at first; I don't want to assume anything when it went fucking south pole the last time, but when she wraps her arms around me, I can't help but lose it. I demand more, and my tongue eases into her perfect mouth; she's eager and ready as she swipes her tongue back into mine. As we explore one another, she groans and I'm a goner. That sound that rumbles from her throat - fucking hell. I want more of her; I need more of her. The kiss makes my stomach flip upside down, and I think this is the most intense and sexually charged kiss I have ever had in my life.

She pulls back and for a second, I think she is going to leave, but she gives me that sultry smile and starts to pull off her dress. "I want you, Adam," she purrs. I think Christmas has come early because this is the best present I have ever wanted. She lets her dress pool on the floor and steps out. I nearly come in my boxers because she is a sight to look at. She's wearing some sort of red silk bra and knickers combo with Christmas trees on. I smile.

Trust Trinity to be wearing Christmas underwear.

I lick my lips, eager to get started, but she stands there with her hands on her hips and a naughty smile. "I've shown you mine now, show me yours," I nearly lose my shit. I pull off my tie eagerly.

Calm down.

I slowly undo the buttons on my shirt. "Wait," she demands, "let me." She walks over and stands before me. I'm desperate to touch her; she hooks her hands under my shirt and gently slides it off. She covers her hands over my chest and places soft kisses there and then rakes her nails down. I can't help but groan. She does this a few times, and it's the best foreplay I have ever had, and she hasn't even touched me properly yet.

I undo my buttons, kick off my shoes, and then trousers. She looks at the tenting bulge in my boxers and nods her head in approval. We stand looking at one another, and all you can hear is our ragged breathing: me in my boxers, Trinity in her Christmas underwear. I mean, this is the line, and I want to cross it so much, but I must wait. I must see if she wants me as much as I want her. I need to hear it; I need to hear it from her mouth.

"Trin," I husk out, "we don't have to do this-"

"Adam, just shut up and fuck me. I can't wait any longer!" she literally pounces on me, and I stumble backwards onto the bed in surprise. Our lips lock in frantic kisses, grinding against each other like naughty teenagers. I roll her onto her back and pull down her bra, her boobs do not disappoint; they're perfect. I circle my tongue over her nipple and bite down gently. I love hearing her moan, I do the same to her other nipple whilst palming the breast with the other hand. She moans again, I pinch and rub, suck, nip and lick. I think these are the best boobs I have ever gotten my mouth around. She sits up, taking off her bra.

"Perfect," I say. She giggles and I plant kisses down her stomach and thread my thumbs through the side of her knickers; she lifts up her perfect arse, and I slide her knickers down her smooth legs. I nip, kiss and swirl my lips all the way back up her legs and then I pull her wet lips apart. I hear her gasp at the contact. Then I make my fantasy of Trinity over the last few weeks come true; I lick, suck and nip her on her soft warm clit, she bucks from the bed with the biggest groan and I can't get enough of that dirty sound, "You're so wet for me, Trinity."

"Adam, if you don't shove your penis inside me right now, I'm going to bloody explode," she demands. I like this side of Trinity. I cover up quickly and nudge her entrance. She looks at me through hooded eyes, her hair messy, and I've never seen anything more beautiful. As I slide slowly into her, the warmth and tingles radiate all over my body; I relish the feeling. I don't want to rush this; I want to take my time, but I don't think my body will let me. I pull all the way out and slowly slide all the way back into the hilt, where we both groan. My fingers are on her nub, working in slow circles. I'm really looking at Trinity, watching her gasps and listening to her moans. The way her breasts move with her short, shallow breaths as I thrust in and out of her, everything screams perfection. It's like we fit together like a puzzle piece; she was what I have been missing all this time, and she has always been right in front of me, but I have been too blind to see.

The build-up comes quickly for both of us; she's getting wetter as my movements become more frantic, deeper and harder. The feelings that are pouring out of me feel uncontrollable. She wants more, and I will give her everything if she'll just let me. Before I know it, I feel her warmth contract against me, and that's all I need to shoot my load deep inside of her. I pull her close, wanting to feel her body on me, with the sweat dripping from both of us. I hold her tight, and it feels fucking great.

The morning after - Trinity

LIAM PAYNE – NAUGHTY LIST

My head feels fuzzy, and my mouth feels a little dry. But that's what happens when I down nearly half a bottle of wine in a short period of time - whilst dealing with the dinner from hell with my psychotic parents. I turn and snuggle up to the warmth, half awake and half asleep. It smells like Adam's aftershave, and I bask in this moment of fantasy before I have to wake up and face reality. I feel a happy ache between my thighs. Moving my hand over the warmth, it meets with some hard-ass-steel abs. I hear the faint sound of another person sleeping. I open one eye, and yep, he's there. I close them again, thinking this isn't real, I will wake up, and it's all a dream. All those years, I dreamt of sleeping with Adam, and this was just another one of them.

Surely?

I squint open my other eye. Nope, he's still there. Shit, shit, shit, mother of all shits, it actually happened.

I semi-ninja roll out of bed and get down on my hands and knees, crawling around his bed, whilst gathering up my clothes. I will laugh at this moment later as I'm half naked, crawling on the floor in Adam's hotel room. My god, we slept together last night, and it was bloody fantastic.

My lady bits sigh again in the happiness of undoubtedly the best night of sex I have ever had. I remember how beautiful it was that Adam stood up for me in front of my parents; I was so turned on by him that it was disgusting.

"Don't do that," Adam croaks. I stop shuffling on the floor and peek up. He sits up slightly, resting on his elbows. He yawns and runs a hand over his stubbly beard, holy shit; he looks like how I dreamt he would look in the morning.

Bloody gorgeous.

His hair is all ruffled, half-closed sleepy eyes, and his chiselled chest in the morning light is something I will cherish in my brain forever. I'm sure this sight will keep me sexually satisfied until I retire. Sleeping together was incredible, but I'm not a naive university student anymore, where it's all rainbows and unicorns and living happily ever after. The real world can suck sometimes, and I can't lose our friendship, so it has to be a mistake.

It is a mistake; the best one I have ever made!

I blame it all on the bloody half a bottle of wine; if I hadn't had that buzz, I would have gone to my bedroom and drowned in my own tears of self-pity. But instead, I went straight to Adam's room. Standing outside his hotel door, I didn't overthink it and just knocked. Now look what's happened. I've been sexually satisfied by the man of my dreams, and nothing will ever measure up to that bitch of an orgasm he gave me.

Fuck!

I even think I can still feel the orgasm now, lingering hours later. With only knickers on, I climb up onto my knees, sort of half cover myself and then perch on the bed, putting my bra on.

"I'm not doing anything!" I squeak. We both know it's a lie and I was definitely trying to escape before he woke up.

Well, that didn't work!

He crawls down the bed and loops his hands around my waist, nuzzling into my neck and kissing it gently. I love the feeling of his hard chest against my back; it makes the butterflies in my stomach take flight over what a real relationship with Adam could look like. I shake the thought away quickly.

It's not real, Trinity.

"We both know you were going to run," he whispers into my hair. I sigh at the fact that he knows me so well, but it's also mixed with a contented sigh as his lips gently skim my neck and all his manly scent is over me again. "Don't go, Trin, stay," he murmurs into my ear. He nips it slightly, then licks my ear lobe and just like that, I want to have sex with him and ride him until New Year's without coming up for breath.

But it can't happen, Trinity; he loves Cora, not you, remember?

I move away from his kisses and turn to face him. He looks sad for a moment, then he turns and puts his glasses on. Ah, jeez, my kryptonite, I'm not going to get any sort of coherent sentence out now with half-naked Superman in my face.

"Adam," I start.

"Trinity," he echoes. He smiles, and I feel all mushy and warm.

Gosh, I don't even know how to say this without sounding like a bitch.

"When I... um... you know you are special to me, right?" I start.

"Oh, fucking hell, Trinity, really?" He literally knows what I'm going to say. Am I so easy to read?

"Don't be mad at me, Adam. You know this can never happen again; we are friends; friends don't fuck without feelings and then what? We ruin our friendship too. I can't go down this road with you. It was a mistake, you know it and I know it," I say it with such conviction, I almost believe it myself. Until my heart feels like it's slowly cracking and my body feels weak.

"Do I?" he asks. He looks really angry, and he's glaring at me as if I just shat on his bed. "Well, you seem to have it all figured out, Trinity, so leave if you need to." He gets off the bed, into the shower room, and slams the door.

Shit. Guess I'm the bitch, then.

It was a mistake - Adam

SAM SMITH – HAVE YOURSELF A MERRY LITTLE XMAS

As I hear Trinity leave the room, I smack my palm on the vanity unit hard and let out a groan. Her words hurt.

It was a mistake.

I have slept with a lot of people over the last few months, just a mindless release, but this was something different. I felt alive again. It felt special. I thought we made a connection last night and I know she felt the same way I did. I really saw it in her eyes, in the way she kissed me - you can't fake that. I'm not one to cuddle, but I needed her close after that, we held each other, and she fell asleep in the crook of my arm. I loved the smell of her tropical scent. I slept well, really well, and it felt right, so what happened in the light of day? When I woke up, I didn't feel the need to ask her to leave, I wanted more of her. I wanted her to stay.

Trinity said it was a mistake, but it didn't feel like a mistake to me. I was so cross with myself and believed that she felt the same way. I let her in, another 'someone' who's fucked with my heart and doesn't want to be with me and wants only to be friends.

I don't get it. I see the way she looks at me now, the carnal urge, the almost kisses, the indirect touches; she has to feel this too. I can't be imagining it, not again.

I change quickly and head down to the hotel gym, I run several kilometres on the treadmill and then beat the shit out of the punching bag until I'm dripping with sweat, and the anger subsides, slightly. We are heading back up to the outskirts of London today for our last two shows. I'm almost tempted to call in sick and jump on a plane and find Charlie. He's gone to Barbados for Christmas – the dipshit. Maybe I just need a break. I look at flights and then curse myself. I'm not one to leave someone in the shit, not Elijah anyway; who would play the guitar for the last few shows?

He would be mega pissed.

If it was someone else, then yeah, but he's been a good friend over the years. So, I resign myself to stay. When the cloud of anger clears, I know that if I had left, that would have meant I was running away too, just like Trinity. I throw my clothes into my bag and head down to the lobby. I see Trinity getting onto the bus; she sees me and gives me that longing look. I know right then that I'm definitely not imagining it; she wants me too - but I think she's scared. So, I decided for the first time in my life that I wanted to stick around in a relationship and fight for her, to make her see that we are worth it.

I climb into the car, knowing being on the bus is not what's best for either of us. Elijah is staring at me. The car pulls out of the car park, and I settle in for the ride back to London. He senses my mood straight away.

"You didn't?" I look at him, confused, and he slaps my head with the back of his hand.

"What the hell, Elijah?" I cover the place he just hit me, and he glares at me. He has a wicked slap, the shithead.

"You shitting slept with her, you idiot!" he shrieks at me crossly. I look at him sheepishly. "You are a dickhead."

"It's not like that," I insist.

"Then Adam, please fucking enlighten me what it's like because if she drops out the last two shows, you're dead to me," he moans.

"I really like her, Elijah, really like her. She's amazing, I don't know why it's taken me so long to realise it. Maybe I am an idiot," I say quietly.

"Then why do you look like someone who has just been told Santa is not real?"

"Because she said it was a mistake," I say sadly. Just saying it out loud hurts just as much as when she said it to me this morning. Elijah barks out a laugh, and I'm pissed at his reaction.

"So let me get this right. You, playboy Adam, finally found someone to tame you, and you got played?" he laughs again, "Sorry, but that's ironic, don't you think?"

"No, just shit." I bang my head against the headrest and groan. "What do I do?"

"Have you talked to her about how you feel?"

"Noooo," I groan again.

"Adam, you are a real shit sometimes," he says, rolling his eyes, "then do that, preferably after the show so you don't ruin it, or you're-"

"Dead, yeah, yeah, I get it," I interrupt.

"Good, now stick some Christmas songs on. I feel like belting out some Wham."

I need time - Trinity

BING CROSBY - WHITE CHRISTMAS

There are only two more shows to get through; that's it. I can do this. Then I can put so much space between Adam and me, and all will be fine; we will laugh about this in a few years' time. It was a moment of weakness; I just knew I couldn't ruin this friendship we had.

I feel scared shitless, I honestly knew I loved him so much it hurt. Everything he did I found attractive: his thoughtfulness, his sense of humour, his beauty, his talent, the way he pushed his glasses up. Now, to add to the list is a mind-blowing orgasm. If I had that every day for the rest of my life, I would be one lucky, satisfied person. He knew his way around the bedroom, the way he touched me last night, his gentle, wanting hands, his calloused rough thumbs from years of playing the guitar pinching my breasts, the way his breath came in short pants when I touched him back. Oh, his penis was moulded for my vagina as he was hitting every erogenous zone in there.

Apparently, I have several – who knew?

The sex was hot and heavy and everything I had ever imagined it to be with him. Such an attentive lover, one might add. I groan in frustration at the whole situation.

But he loves Cora; he always will; I won't be his pity kiss or fuck.

I half hoped he would come on the bus so we could chat about it. What I said this morning was shit, and I feel guilty and stupid. He wanted me to stay, but my insecurities made me run away. I guess he's doing that, too, now as well.

I deserve the silent treatment from him.

I sit at the back of the bus this time, hiding away from everyone else, especially Ben and Elle, who seem to be finger fucking at the table seat, and I internally vom. I stick in my earbuds, connect to my phone and listen to some nice musical classics to soothe my racing microwave thoughts as they go round and round my head.

Christmas is only three days away, and I question whether I can stand a Christmas on my own. I have so many emotions running around my heart that it feels dangerous to be alone. Going to my parents isn't an option; they had left a voicemail demanding what my outburst at dinner was the other night. But that fight is for another day; I don't think they will ever understand how they make me feel, but for now, I have said something back, and that is a start. When I feel a little bit stronger, I will tell them everything about how they make me feel. If it makes our bond stronger, great, but if this is it, then I have to be okay with that, too. All I know is I can't carry on this narcissistic and abusive mental relationship with them anymore.

I deserve better.

Maybe if it gets too much, I could go to Cora's and Zach's for Christmas. But then I remember she is over six months pregnant, and with her baby due in only three months, this will be the last Christmas they get together as a family of three. Not that she would say anything if I did come, but maybe I could go on Boxing Day?

My thoughts circle back to Adam and me. Can I see a relationship with Adam? It's all I ever wanted, but I hadn't even asked if he wanted to be with me. In fact, I don't know how he even feels, and it's not like I have been honest with him either. I now feel like an idiot. He's not a mind reader; maybe he thinks I only wanted a quick shag.

Shit.

I have to talk to him, that's the best thing. Even if he is in love with my best friend, Cora – this talk needs to happen. Great, I've made a plan. I feel more settled that I have made a decision and doze the rest of the journey.

I'm awoken by a jolt indicating that we have parked up at the theatre in Stratford. As I put my phone in my bag, I see that a text has come through from Cora, saying that she'll be coming to see me at my last show and she can't wait. My stomach twists in knots; Cora and Adam will finally see each other again.

Fuck. Now I need a new plan.

The last show - Trinity

SIA — SNOWMAN

I know I always feel nervous when my parents are coming to see me, but this was on another level; I feel sick to my stomach now. I hadn't mentioned to Adam that Cora was in the audience tonight. It's ridiculous, really, but my irrational thoughts keep on coming through, and I'm scared that he will realise that when he sees Cora again, he actually still wants Cora and not me. They hadn't seen or spoken to one another since Cora's wedding. Cora has no idea why she has had the silent treatment from Adam.

Tonight, his true feelings will be revealed and I will see how much he is in love with her, still. Then, my heart will shatter into a million pieces. This time, I'm not sure I will ever recover from him. I keep seeing him glance at me with worry plastered all over his face. I hate myself for feeling so insecure about how I feel or how others perceive this. But when I watched Cora and Adam's broken love story unfold in front of my eyes for so many years - my heart is right to be cautious.

As we sit to play the show, my hands are clammy, my heart hurts from beating so fast for so long, and I feel aware of sounds and voices. But I can't concentrate, like an out-of-body experience, a car crash of a disaster just waiting to happen. I keep my head down and play as best as I can.

I take a peek at the interval, and they've literally snagged the first row; Cora can see me now, and she beams wildly at me. Cora's with Zach, her husband, and her sister Daisy is here with a man I've never seen before, but she seems cross about it. I see that Sophie and her boyfriend Oliver are here too and give them a wave. I then put two and two together. Oliver used to be on a show called 'Always Famous', and the other guy was Toby – wow, the TV show did not do him enough justice; he was beautiful.

I notice quite a few of the audience members also agreed, as when Daisy gestures wildly at him and then walks away, he follows shortly after her with a few head turns of ogling Toby's backside.

I glance back at Adam, and he follows my line of sight; he can see Cora now, too. I watch closely like a lunatic; he gives her a small wave and then darts his eyes back to me as if he's pieced this disastrous event together and understands my anxiety-ridden face for most of the day. His eyes glower at me and I feel like I've been a naughty child, and he shakes his head to the side as if he is disappointed in me. I'm disappointed in myself if I'm being really honest; I've acted insane today and usually, I feel quite level-headed. All I know is that I don't want to be in the same vicinity when they come face to face.

The rest of the show seems to go by in a blur. Putting on this brave face is exhausting; the minutes drag regardless. When the show ends, people are happy and excited about a job well done, and they discuss where they are all going to go out tonight. All I want to do is crawl into a hole and hibernate for the whole winter to get over this mess. I fake some sort of illness and say that I can't join them, but I do tell them to keep in touch as we all pack away the equipment.

Cora comes over to the orchestra pit and congratulates us all on a wonderful show, and says she'll meet us backstage. Of course, with her reputation, she knows bloody everyone within the London Arts community, so there's no escaping this now. As I pack up and walk by Adam, he grabs my hand gently.

"Can we talk?" he asks hopefully.

"I don't know if now is the right time," he releases my hand, and his face falls a bit. I head over to put the equipment back on the bus. When I walk through the halls backstage, Cora envelopes me in the biggest hug, peppering me with kisses and saying how brilliant I was. I hug Zach as well and then stroke her growing bump.

"He's a wriggler," she announces proudly. I gush over how beautiful she looks, and Zach holds her tightly in agreement. "We can't stop long, as we have to get the last train home."

Then it all happens. I almost run, but fear and intrigue keep me routed to my spot. Adam comes through the hallway, and oddly, I even see Zach tense slightly. But as soon as Adam approaches us, he opens the palm of his hand and shakes Adam's hand warmly. Cora literally strangles him in a hug. Telling him off for not returning her calls, he mutters how busy he has been. Which we all know is a lie, unless you mean sleeping with most of London, then yes, he has been busy. I can now be added to that list. With that thought, I seem to blush, remembering how amazing he is in bed.

Bloody hell, Trinity, get a grip.

Zach's phone rings; he looks at the caller ID and sighs. "I will be back," he kisses Cora on the head and walks off down the hall.

So, the three of us are standing there in awkward silence. What do I say? I don't think anything positive or coherent is going to come out. I shuffle my feet and Cora looks between us both, eyes narrowed.

"Trinity, can I borrow you?" Elijah bellows from the side. This is now my other nightmare coming true, leaving them alone together. I bite my lip, and Adam's gaze drops down and notices this; he frowns. I hug Cora goodbye.

"I will see you at New Year, okay?" Cora tells me, and I nod as I walk away. I don't say bye to Adam, I know what happens next. He looks at her adoringly and remembers that she still makes all his dreams come true.

Elijah is at the other end of the hallway. We chat briefly and he offers me another position starting after Easter. A Broadway show he is co-directing, and one of his violinists has dropped out due to medical reasons. It's a one-year contract, and I happily take it. This is the breakthrough I've been looking for. A steady job and an income for a year, what a relief! As I go to leave, I glance back to where I see Adam and Cora, who are still talking. She's smiling so hard, they're holding hands, and his eyes are alight like she's the best thing ever. And there it is; my heart is crushed again. I couldn't have saved myself from this. I fell so hard for Adam, and then I crashed and burned.

Merry fucking Christmas.

The last show - Adam

JUSTIN BIEBER - MISTLETOE

This tour has been surprising and frustrating in more ways than one, but all around, it has been a good few weeks. To say this was a favour to Elijah, I have enjoyed myself.

Until tonight.

Something is seriously wrong with Trinity; she is bouncing her leg so hard I think she might take off, biting her lip; she is more than anxious tonight. I keep on thinking it's me, with what happened between us last night, and I feel terrible. As soon as the show finishes, I'm going to wrap my arms around her and make sure she is okay, even I'm feeling her tension from several seats away.

At interval time, I suddenly put two and two together. I watch as Trinity peeks over the top at someone; she never peaks, always professional, with her tight black jeans and frilly black top. When I look over and see Cora is here, my heart literally stops.

Now I know why Trinity is worried.

She had aired her concern, when we first kissed, about me being in love with Cora still and how Trinity was a pity kiss. But it wasn't like that at all. Yes, I was heartbroken months ago, but Trinity had pulled it all out of me over the last few weeks. That moment after she sang my song and we kissed changed everything. Trinity is all I can see now. So, my heart stopped as I knew I had to face my past and be honest with myself. There was no more hiding from Cora. She didn't even know why we weren't talking, and I felt like a shit friend because of that. I sadly smiled at her.

After the show, I try to talk to Trinity, but she brushes me off. After I have taken my guitar back to the bus, I see Trinity and Cora talking.

It is now or never.

When I see Cora backstage, I feel nothing, and it's a relief. I am so over this obsession, and I feel happier and lighter. All I can see is the worry in Trinity's eyes and the tension in her body, I couldn't understand why. All I wanted to do was kiss the shit out of Trinity and tell her what she meant to me, and she wouldn't let me get a word in.

"Trinity, can I borrow you?" Elijah shouts. I turn and see his shit-eating grin; he knows what is happening here and he will pay for this. Trinity leaves without saying goodbye.

"What's happened?" Cora gives me the stare when Trin is out of earshot. I blow out a breath.

Here goes nothing.

"Cora, I need to apologise; I blocked you from my life because I was gutted you married Zach," I admit.

"What, why?" she looks shocked.

"Because I fell in love with you," I look down at my feet and shift them a little in embarrassment because this conversation is years too late.

"Oh," she sounds surprised, "Oh," she whispers sadly. "Adam-"

"Let me finish. I needed space from everything and then got thrown into this show, which made me realise what a mess I have been over you. I didn't know Trinity was here, playing in the show," I say.

"Well, if you picked up your phone, I could of blooming told you, you shite," she responds sarcastically.

I chuckle. "My heart healed and I fell in love with Trin," Cora nearly squeals, jumping up and down and then holding her bump at the over-zealous gesture. She's practically beaming at me. "I really love her, Cora. Trinity is everything I want in a person, and she can't see it. She thinks I will only love you until I die and that she's my pity, my rebound. When she's not, she's amazing in so many ways I can't describe," she pulls my hands into hers.

"You know she loves you too, right?" I look at the happiness and sparkle in her eyes that mirror mine.

"Has she said that to you?" I ask hopefully.

"Nope, but she told Daisy, who told me, and if you ever tell her I told you that, I will kill you as pregnancy rage is a thing. Look, I'm telling you and being a shite to my best friend because I think this is the push you need to go get her," she smiles proudly at me.

I hug her carefully, "Congratulations, by the way," I say and she rubs her bump instinctively.

"Thanks, Adam, and I am really sorry; I didn't know how you felt. I mean, I'm not sure what I could have done, but you know?" she smiles sadly at me.

I smile back at her, "I'm over it."

Now, I need to find Trinity.

Christmas Eve - Trinity

LEONA LEWIS – ONE MORE SLEEP

I didn't go home last night; I couldn't face it. Plus, it takes several hours to warm my place up and with the heating being off for weeks in December, it will be like the arctic tundra. So, I decided to stay in the hotel the show provided - I told everyone else I had gone home ill whilst they went out and partied. I wanted to bask in all the shows I had performed in over the last few weeks. I have loved every minute of it, the highs and the lows. I wanted to ride that artistic high and be proud of what I have achieved – and I got a job out of it, too. Plus, the hotel had a hot, bubbly bath. I didn't have a bath in my flat, and I really wanted one. I climbed into the warmth, relaxed my tired muscles and cried. I stayed in there for hours, eating chocolate and drinking wine – soothing my broken heart.

Maybe Mum was right, and I did have a drinking problem.

When my skin was shrivelled and pruned, screaming at me that my skin may turn to mush, I climbed into the warm, fluffy bed and watched re-runs of 'Vampire Diaries'. There's nothing like beautiful men and women, blood, gore and romance to send you off into a blissful sleep.

When I wake up, it's quite early so I head back with my suitcase on the tube. The weather is a bag of crap. I shiver most of the way home, and as soon as I enter my cold, empty flat, I turn the heating on, put in a load of washing, then head off to the coffee shop for the day to inhale a spiced latte and a ginger biscuit.

I love Christmas Eve, despite having to spend this one alone.

I catch up on emails. I read a very long email and script from Elijah and try to focus on my next role. As the cloudy day turns into a cloudy night, I head back home, soaking in the Christmas spirit. Everyone wishes me a Merry Christmas as they pass with happy smiles, and even carollers are on the street corner, which I definitely stop and watch whilst still shivering from the cold.

My flat, thankfully, is a lot warmer. I put the washing out, put the Christmas lights on, which hang loosely around the tree and look at my pitiful three presents under there – one from my parents, one from Will and one from Cora. I miss that feeling as a child when you wake up Christmas morning to piles of presents under the tree, the anticipation of Santa and the house full of family.

I dress in my Giraffe pyjamas, put on a classic 'Muppets Christmas Carol,' crack open another bottle of wine and settle in for the evening. Before I can even get comfy, there's a knock on the door. I hadn't even ordered takeout yet. I wondered if Jaz had locked himself out of his flat again; it's happened countless times. The knock comes again louder.

"Yes, I'm coming," I shout as I push myself off the settee, pad across the room in my fluffy slippers and fling open the door. I breathe in a small gasp. There he is, in all his gorgeous glory, standing outside my door, his arms spread across the door frame, looking down at the floor. Finally, he looks under his eyelashes and glowers up at me.

"You ran again," he says. I cross my arms over my chest, and he smiles, "Nice pyjamas."

"I like them," he smirks.

"Why do you keep running away, Trinity?" he asks.

"I'm not ru-" I stop myself as he arches his eyebrow. I was running. We both know it.

"Can I come in?" he rights himself up to my level. He has cut his hair shorter; his tight grey t-shirt enhances his muscles and well, his tight jeans aren't hiding much, again.

Stop looking at his crotch, weirdo!

"No," I look into his eyes and try not to melt under his gaze.

"No, why?"

"Because I'm busy," I declare. He looks over my shoulder, assessing my busyness, which again is a full-on lie.

"Wine, chocolate and a movie, great, what are we watching?" he says playfully as he scoots around me and lets himself in. I stand there for a second and have no idea what to do. I shut the door as he plonks himself on the settee, kicks off his trainers and puts his feet on the table. He takes a sip of my wine and helps himself to the chocolate - my chocolate. "Muppets Christmas Carol? Timeless. I remember watching this on repeat as a kid. It's Marley and Marley, wooooooooo," he laughs, and I find myself laughing too. I grab another glass, sit on the armchair, not wanting to be too close to him and pour myself another glass of red.

He's engrossed in the movie; I know what he's trying to do. He's trying to alleviate the tension in this room, and move past whatever he did or said to Cora. But the tension is still there, as thick as ever. I sit there and stare at him, waiting for him to talk. But all I can really think about is his experienced hands over my body, his perfect dick inside me, and then the way he looked at Cora last night, which then shatters my fantasy. I look away, the hurt bubbling inside of me.

"Trinity, if you don't tell me what's going on in your pretty head, I'm going to come over there and fuck it out of you," I look at his playful eyes and his dirty words have me all turned on. I don't know how he does this to me. I want to be angry at him, I do, but the thought of him fucking me senseless also sounds great. I whimper a little, "Trin," he warns through gritted teeth.

"I saw you," I blurt out.

"You saw me what?" he asks confused.

"With Cora." He furrows his eyebrows at what I'm saying. "After I finished speaking with Elijah, I saw you in the corridor. You were holding hands, and you both looked so happy. I can't do this to myself, Adam. I can't love you like this anymore. I can't be friends with you anymore, so I need you to leave."

Christmas Eve - Adam

MARIAH CAREY - ALL I WANT FOR CHRISTMAS IS YOU

I look at her crossly. I am thinking back to the interaction with Cora in the corridor. What she saw was me telling Cora how much I loved Trinity. I nearly burst out laughing, but I hold it in, then I'm angry because assumption is a bitch.

"Can you hear yourself?" I bark.

"Yes, and it is absolutely insane, but that's how you make me feel, Adam. I can't control the way I am with you. I'm angry and jealous of everything and I can't stop that. You love Cora, I can't have you, I can't seem to want anyone else. What the hell am I supposed to do?"

She looks defeated, and her eyes are glassy from unshed tears. Her honest outburst fills me up. She loves me and wants me. I knew she did, but to actually hear it from her mouth is all I need. I move off the settee and kneel down in front of her as she's sat on the armchair. I take her hands in mine; she tries to pull away, but I hold them tighter.

"Adam, don't. Just please leave," she whispers and looks away.

"No, let me tell you what I was discussing with Cora," I say adamantly.

"I don't want to hear it," I guide her face gently to look at me.

"You can and you will," she lets out a soft whimper to my demand. "I was talking about you."

"Please, Adam, stop," a tear falls from her face, and I cup her cheek.

"I was telling Cora that I was in love with you," her glassy eyes focus on mine; she bites her lip and the crease in her forehead appears.

"What?"

"If you don't believe me, ring her, text, I don't care, whatever confirmation you need to stop yourself from thinking anything else. But know this, Trinity, I love you, I want you, I want everything from you," she gasps as she realises what I am confessing to her. I let go of her cheek and place my hand on hers. "I want you, Trinity."

"I don't know what to say," she murmurs with disbelief.

"You don't need to say anything," with that, I push up onto my knees, kissing her firmly on the lips, tasting her salty tears. Honestly, I think if I kissed her in the doorway, she wouldn't have said no.

I stand and pull her off the armchair, I sit down on the settee and she climbs on top of me, which is great because her boobs are literally in my face.

Well, hello boys, I remember them oh so well last time.

She lets out a deep sigh as she feels how hard I am for her. I swipe my tongue into her mouth, no soft kisses, just straight into the good stuff. I love the throaty groan she makes; it shoots to my dick, who stands to attention. I think he's so ready he's almost doing a salute as well!

Trinity is grinding on top of me as I use my greedy hands to hold her perfect arse. My hands then travel under her pyjamas, grateful there's no bra there so that I have easy access to her perfect boobs. They feel soft and her nipples are so erect, she groans in her mouth as I swirl my thumb around them. Before I know it, she's undone her buttons and discarded the pyjama top. I lean back a little to appraise her beauty. I palm her breasts, leaning forward, swivelling my tongue along her nipple, sucking down gently, eliciting another groan. I think right now that is my favourite noise from her mouth.

She moves her lips to my neck, kissing and licking behind my ear and fuck me, it feels good. Trinity threads her finger through my hair, with her nails slightly scraping along the surface, which then has me groaning. Such a simple touch but it has me shivering in anticipation of her next move; it's so sexy. She pulls off my jumper and then my tee shirt, taking her time to kiss my chest with soft touches and her plump lips.

She's moving slowly down my body and is now on her knees before me with a naughty look in her eye. She unbuttons my jeans and pulls them down along with my boxers. She then licks my balls from base to tip and fuck me, she's good. As she takes me in her mouth, the wetness, the tightness of her mouth has me groaning, cursing myself we should have started all this at university. Trinity is vigorous with her hands moving up and down my length while her mouth sucks and licks. I love the feeling of her all over me. When she slows a little, licking the tip of my dick, I lean forward and pull her back onto my lap. My mouth finds hers immediately, tasting my own arousal on her lips and shit me that's hot.

"Wait, I need to get a condom," I whisper breathlessly.

"Are you clean?" I look into the darkness of her eyes and realise what she's asking me.

"Yes," I admit.

"I'm on the pill and...I've never gone without a condom before," her words fill my heart with pride.

"Me either," I confess as I pull her thong to one side and nudge myself inside her. We're both still for a moment, and then I push myself fully into her as she leans in and holds me. I pull her hair to one side and gently kiss her neck. I start a slow, deep rhythm, her warmth spreads over my body of how good she feels without a condom. It feels more intimate, and the intense feeling is not lost on me. Having sex like this is on another level; I feel everything so much more that I have to calm my thoughts – no one wants a man to finish this early.

As she raises her body up and down onto me, I take the opportunity to worship her breasts, licking and sucking. Her breathing is becoming more laboured, and her pants are coming faster as we move against one another deeper and harder. I hold her around her body to lie her down on the sofa and thrust so deep and fast, that she gasps with delight, pulling me into the most amazing kiss. As I continue my relentless rhythm, I feel her tighten around me, I look at her face as she closes her eyes, watching her orgasm and with that, I come deep inside her wetness. Claiming her as mine. I slow and pulse inside her as I breathe Trinity in on my release. She kisses me again and holds me close.

"I love you, Adam Turner," she whispers in my ear.

Christmas Day - Trinity

SHAKIN' STEVENS – MERRY CHRISTMAS EVERYONE

I wake up to Adam in my arms and it is the best feeling ever. We are finally going to do this. I mean, I'm not sure what this is, as nothing has been discussed, regardless we are doing this. He told me he loved me last night; he loves me and that's something amazing I never thought I would hear come out of his mouth. Well, apart from him moaning my name when he came inside me.

That was pretty fantastic, too.

Last night was amazing; we had sex in the front room, again in the bathroom and some very slow and mind-blowing sex in my bed as well. My vagina feels sore and if he dares to come near me with his massive dick again today, I may fake a headache or a period because I need time to recover from that amazing sex session. I roll over and check the time on my phone. It's 11:30 a.m. and I slept through. I haven't slept properly in days; I definitely needed it and sleeping in Adam's arms was wonderful.

I see a text has come through from Cora.

'Happy Christmas, you beautiful woman; I'm hoping that Adam came to tell you how in love with you he is. If he hasn't, what a shite. But it's true, he told me how much he loves you, now sort it out, you silly bitch, love you!'

Not that I was going to check in and ask, but she knew I needed the reassurance. I'm so glad my bestie knows me well enough to send a message like that. I put my phone back on the side table, thinking back to that moment. So, what I saw the other night was him confessing his love for me; it felt strange to hear that from him. Adam loves me, he loves me and I liked how easily it rolled off the tongue. I liked the feeling. They say love blooms in the strangest places, and I had wanted him for so long, it didn't feel real, like I was going to wake up from a dream really soon. Except this wasn't a dream, he was really here, in my bedroom, in my bed, naked. My room even smelt like him and sex. I snuggle closer to him, and he holds me tighter; he's half-awake and I see him smirk.

"You didn't run," he croaks out and kisses my hair.

"Neither did you," I hear a grumbly laugh, and I gently trace his smooth, chiselled chest with my fingertips, enjoying this moment of quiet between him and I. He hums a happy noise at my touch.

"I could get used to this," I smile at his tender words as he gives out a long sigh of happiness. He eases out of my hold and rolls onto his side, putting his glasses on, and oh my, next time, he needs to keep the glasses on when we have sex. I wonder if he's into role-play. "Merry Christmas, Trinity," he kisses me gently on my lips.

"Merry Christmas, Adam," I smile at him feeling happy and for once, content. He moves out of bed.

"I'm going to have a shower and then we can go out for a walk. You're welcome to join me in the shower," he flirts, waggling his eyebrows and pointing to his now erect penis. I laugh.

"God no, my vagina is broken," he laughs, going into the bathroom, "I will put some coffee on," I hear the shower turn on and get out of bed. Pulling on my pyjamas and a dressing gown because the heating is off, it is again like the arctic tundra in my flat. I flick the heating on and start brewing a pot of coffee.

Christmas Day - Adam

KELLY CLARKSON – UNDERNEATH THE TREE

I wake up to Trinity in my arms, and it is the best feeling in the world. She didn't try to run; she stayed, and last night was confirmation of even better things to come. Once we are both showered, breakfast consumed, and have drunk three cups of coffee, we are ready to go. We would have gone for a walk a lot earlier, but we make out a hell of a lot more, which makes me want to fuck her again and worship her body. But she lets out a little yelp, claiming that her vagina is still broken and needs a little more rest. So, we decided to go for a walk to calm our dirty desires. But later, broken or not, I'm going to worship her body; my dick can rest easy because it will all be tongue; I'm going to kiss and lick her better.

As we leave her flat, I notice sellotaped to the fridge door there's a picture of me in the gym, top off. I pull it off and put it in her hand.

"We can talk about this one later?"

"Oh fuck, Adam," she looks so embarrassed.

I smile. "Did you used to play with yourself to me? Have you printed more pictures of things like this?"

Her beetroot face is all I need as confirmation she totally has and we are so exploring that thought later. We walk down the stairs and I pat my coat pocket to reassure myself it's still there. I have a present for her, and I'm not sure how she is going to feel about it.

Bundled up in our coats, hats, scarves and gloves, we walk out into the cold Christmas afternoon air. She doesn't realise where we are going, but I know she loves going to the place I picked. She used to drag me there every Christmas holiday when we were at university. Unfortunately, it's going to be a long walk; Trinity hates walking for long periods of time. After some serious moaning from her, some piggyback rides from me and almost an hour later, we reach our destination - even the takeaway coffees from her flat are not lifting her mood.

As the snow starts to fall, I couldn't plan this any better; Trinity lets out a little happy squeal and pulls me closer as we walk into Covent Garden. Her eyes alight as she realises where we are; she admires the decorations and the lights on the humongous Christmas tree.

"You remembered! I haven't had time to come here yet," she beams at me, pulling me into a hug. "I do love the lights," she adds. I smile back at her, knowing how much I bloody love this girl and how I'm going to spend every day telling and showing her. I like how quiet it is here; there aren't many people about it as we share a special moment together. I start to feel a bit of a chicken, and my stomach does a nervous flip - but I know I can do this. I know how I feel about her, and I'm not wasting another moment, so I pull out the box from my coat pocket and get down on the wet, sleety ground. It takes her a moment to look down and notice what I'm doing, and she looks at me a little angry.

"Adam!" she shrieks. "No, I'm not going to marry you, you idiot. You only realised you loved me yesterday and now you want to get married. What the hell is wrong with you?" she blows out air from her mouth, and her eyebrows are so far up her forehead I think they might take off. I love it when she's feisty.

I bark out a laugh.

I don't move from the ground despite my kneecaps being cold and wet. "Trinity, I have loved you since the first time I met you – although I didn't quite know it at first but I frigging do now. Through the years, that has grown into something I couldn't even describe now. I didn't understand what to make of it, not at first. Not until you were singing to me in my hotel room, and it hit me so hard. Granted, the nakedness and sex helped, too. You are my best friend, you make me laugh, you are sexy as hell, and I want to have beautiful babies with you. I mean, not right now, but I would like to practice lots!" I hold her hand and smile at her, and she returns it with her warm smile. "The thought of not being with you every day, makes my heart ache because I want all of that; I want it all with you. I love you, Trinity."

"That was corny as shit. But beautiful. I'm still not marrying you, though, so get up. This is ridiculous," she laughs. I get up from the floor and open the box to her and smirk. She looks at the ring confused and then back at me.

"But it's not an engagement ring- because I knew you would say no. Instead, I've gone American style and got you a promise ring. This ring says you're mine, and I am yours, and I promise by the end of next year, you will be my wife because I've waited so long for you, for this, for us, and I'm not going away. So, no, I'm not asking you to marry me, not right now," I say as I push the ring on her finger, "I'm promising it."

And they lived happily ever after?

QUEEN — THANK GOD IT'S CHRISTMAS

...Or at least for Christmas, because you know, it's life and shit gets real!

Acknowledgements

Thank you as always to Anna and Lisa for editing this book and saving my ass yet again - you are both so awesome. Paige, you are amazing at writing another stellar playlist and thank you for reading this story of Adam and Trinity.

I really enjoyed writing this story, this one flowed so well and anyone will tell you how much I love a romance with a happy ending or in a Christmas movie, it's like a personal satisfaction. I love Christmas.

The Playlist

Chapter 1: Good Goodbye - Linkin Park https://open.spotify.com/track/650OeHTLxZAQmb4aEbGmaA

Chapter 2: Christmas Time – Backstreet Boys https://open.spotify.com/track/02tPqiXPgZWca1UrWKrkln

Chapter 3: Baby Please Come Home – Cher https://open.spotify.com/track/4kcXZH4jWafsgd7RMSKLYw

Chapter 4: Santa Tell Me – Ariana Grande https://open.spotify.com/track/62AGBURrH2EsqA7yblCGXP

Chapter 5: Fairytale of New York - The Pogues https://open.spotify.com/track/3VTNVsTTu05dmTsVFrmGpK

Chapter 6: Christmas Lights – Coldplay https://open.spotify.com/track/3ODH5TiKxbhJ0y1sFGZpd7

Chapter 7: Rocking Around the Christmas Tree – Justin Bieber https://open.spotify.com/track/4mEm3ggvifnQuUOqPvDWPp

Chapter 8: I Saw Mommy Kissing Santa Claus – Jackson 5 https://open.spotify.com/track/15sxLiiChE5dCW3Y756oas

Chapter 9: Santa Baby – Kylie Minogue https://open.spotify.com/track/0cM5URUqqQTpJWonmdzF1J

Chapter 10: It's the Most Wonderful Time of the Year – Andy Williams https://open.spotify.com/track/5hslUAKq9I9CG2bAulFkHN

Chapter 11: Baby It's Cold Outside – Idina Menzel https://open.spotify.com/track/0Ie5uiv54KgCr7P4sYDTHl

Chapter 12: Lonely This Christmas – KT Tunstall https://open.spotify.com/track/1N2SnyLc8phjWyG6J3lT3Y

Chapter 13: Last Christmas – Wham https://open.spotify.com/track/2FRnf9qhLbvw8fu4IBXx78

Chapter 14: Under the Mistletoe – Sia https://open.spotify.com/track/7IoBw5SWava4CDQ2mJCvsa

Chapter 15: Wrapped In Red – Kelly Clarkson https://open.spotify.com/track/2nMZx7QHerfo4Wv37xNUEC

Chapter 16: Christmas Without You – Ava Max https://open.spotify.com/track/1QLZKzC2pjP4ySf4ALrNhm

Chapter 17: Christmas Isn't Cancelled (Just You) – Kelly Clarkson https://open.spotify.com/track/4zHDuDQx8dcWVmVVtyIzRO

Chapter 18: Blame It on the Mistletoe – Ella Henderson https://open.spotify.com/track/0lIhytBQ9DWenT3BNkhCem

Chapter 19: Naughty List – Liam Payne https://open.spotify.com/track/2G5f6e2kxGOJsztnR3s5Ty

Chapter 20: Have Yourself A Merry Little Xmas – Sam Smith https://open.spotify.com/track/1AcH4HyHBsXXv3YExawMNC

Chapter 21: White Christmas – Bing Crosby https://open.spotify.com/track/4so0Wek9Ig1p6CRCHuINwW

Chapter 22: Snowman – Sia https://open.spotify.com/track/7uoFMmxln0GPXQ0AcCBXRq

Chapter 23: Mistletoe – Justin Bieber https://open.spotify.com/track/7xapw9Oy21WpfEcib2ErSA

Chapter 24: One More Sleep – Leona Lewis https://open.spotify.com/track/78pn8k7RogKo2oxl0DyX6d

Chapter 25: All I Want for Christmas Is You – Mariah Carey https://open.spotify.com/track/0bYg9bo50gSsH3LtXe2SQn

Chapter 26: Merry Christmas Everyone – Shakin' Stevens https://open.spotify.com/track/2TE4xW3ImvpltVU0cPcKUn

Chapter 27: Underneath the Tree – Kelly Clarkson https://open.spotify.com/track/3nAp4IvdMPPWEH9uuXFFV5

Chapter 28: Thank God It's Christmas — Queen https://open.spotify.com/track/0QtJZpyfZF67QF32p41NXa

Printed in Great Britain
by Amazon

57996973R00067